A sharp crack shattered his sleep.

Miguel shouted and sat bolt upright, pain gouging his side. He clutched himself, groaning, thinking he'd been shot again. Quick light filled the room and was gone before he got his bearings.

"Miguel," a soft voice called. "Miguel, it's all right. It's the storm."

"Veronica?"

"Yes," she whispered.

"I've been...shot." He lay back on the pillow. "My own people...shot me."

"No, Miguel," she said, her soothing voice gradually calming his dream-muddled mind. "Guerrero's people shot you. Are you okay? Did you—?"

"It happened again."

"You were dreaming." She stroked his face and found him feverish.

Miguel couldn't let her leave him. The reality had been a nightmare, and now the nightmare seemed absolutely real. "Would you mind if I held you?"

"No," she said quietly. "I wouldn't mind at all."

Dear Reader,

Once again, Silhouette Intimate Moments has lined up a stellar list of authors. This month's books are sure to go straight to your heart.

Start off with *Mackenzie's Mountain*, Linda Howard's long-awaited return to the line. This story of a prim and proper schoolteacher who learns about passion from tough loner Wolf Mackenzie will live in your mind long after you turn the last page. With her talent for drama and passion, Linda brings her characters to life in a way few authors can match.

Kathleen Eagle makes a final trip back to the island of De Colores this month in *Paintbox Morning*. You may remember Miguel Hidalgo from the earlier books in the series, but even if you don't, I know you will never forget him once you've read this story of triumph and tenderness.

Doreen Owens Malek is back with *A Marriage of Convenience*, a new twist on an old theme. And Paula Detmer Riggs, though a relative newcomer, shows why she has quickly become so popular with *Desperate Measures*, a suspenseful tale of love's lessons learned.

In coming months, look out for more of the authors you've come to expect from Silhouette Intimate Moments, authors like Kathleen Creighton, Marilyn Pappano, Heather Graham Pozzessere and Nora Roberts. Their books will take you away to a world where love is perfect and dreams do come true—and isn't that a place we'd all like to be?

Leslie J. Wainger
Senior Editor
Silhouette Books

Kathleen Eagle
Paintbox Morning

Silhouette Intimate Moments
Published by Silhouette Books New York
America's Publisher of Contemporary Romance

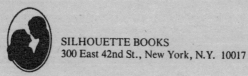

SILHOUETTE BOOKS
300 East 42nd St., New York, N.Y. 10017

ISBN: 0-373-07284-8

First Silhouette Books printing April 1989

Printed in the U.S.A.

Books by Kathleen Eagle

Silhouette Special Edition

Someday Soon #204
A Class Act #274
Georgia Nights #304
Something Worth Keeping #359
Carved in Stone #396
Candles in the Night #437

Silhouette Intimate Moments

For Old Times' Sake #148
More Than a Miracle #242
But That Was Yesterday #257
Paintbox Morning #284

KATHLEEN EAGLE

is a transplant from Massachusetts to her favorite regional setting, the Dakota prairie. As educator, wife, mother and writer, she believes that a woman's place is wherever she's needed—and anywhere she needs to be.

For my sister, Jill.
It's going to be a bright, sunshiny day.

Prologue

The bright white glare from the noonday sun was almost as troublesome as the man who persisted in poking the barrel of a pistol in Miguel Hidalgo's back. Miguel's eyes were light-sensitive, and he had lost his sunglasses. And now it appeared that his sensitivity to .44-caliber bullets was about to be tested. He knew his skin would puncture as easily as Julius Caesar's, although the three men who accompanied him in his final walk were hardly senators. The island's fledgling government had not advanced that far.

Miguel paused to turn his face to the salty breeze. His escort prodded him between the shoulder blades, and they continued on. His senses were heightened now, and he wanted to absorb an overdose of his island home—the rhythm of gently lapping waves, the gritty feeling of sand in his shoes, the smell of hibiscus and seawater and the sun-bronzed face of his fellow islanders. Even the three who were bent on killing him.

They were young enough to be idealistic but possessed of enough naïveté to be totally misdirected. They were soldiers, and they had their orders. They had chosen to put their trust in the man who appeared to be the stronger, a man whose very name was a threat. Rodolfo Guerrero would soon claim to be the solitary authority in De Colores. Miguel remembered the beginning of it all—the three of them: Castillo, Guerrero and Hidalgo. Suddenly Castillo was dead, and Guerrero was clearly wasting no time ridding himself of his other partner. Miguel's dying regret would be that he was leaving his little homeland in the clutches of a tyrant.

The stretch of sand became rocky as they approached the cliffs. With his hands tied behind him, Miguel's balance was unreliable. He cursed the smooth soles of his shoes as he negotiated the rocks. When he stumbled, one of the soldiers reached reflexively to steady him, while another jabbed him in the side with a pistol. "Move along," their companion ordered.

"Where are you taking me?"

Miguel's question was ignored until they stood beneath the dark cliffs, and the man who held the gun to his back announced, "This is far enough."

They spun him so that his back was to the sea. The man who held him at gunpoint had a lean face and hungry eyes. He gave an impatient wave with his pistol, and the other two clutched at Miguel's shoulders like a pair of buzzards and ripped the oak-leaf clusters from his khaki shirt. To Miguel the rank had always been a sham, and he was relieved to feel the weight of it lifted from his shoulders. He had shunned the ribbons and gold braid with which Guerrero had decorated himself so generously. But when the small embroidered shield bearing the rainbow-hued emblem of De Colores was torn from its place above his breast pocket, he flinched.

"Why are you doing this?" he demanded.

"We are ordered to strip you of all symbols of the country you betrayed," said the man behind the gun.

"Betrayed?" Miguel's blood heated at the sound of the word. "*Betrayed!* I may be guilty of many sins, but not treason." He looked from one anxious young face to another. "Am I to be tried here on the beach? Is this Guerrero's latest idea of judicial process?"

"You have already been found guilty, *señor*. We do not question the general's orders."

"'*Señor*,' is it?" Miguel gave a short, mirthless laugh. "And Colonel Guerrero has promoted himself to general. Is there a promotion in this for the three of you, as well?" Miguel read the answer in their silence and suggested quietly, "Beware of rank that comes too easily. You see how easily it may be stripped away."

The lean-faced soldier jerked his head, and the other two moved away from Miguel as they pocketed the bits of metal and cloth they'd torn from his clothes. Then they unsnapped their holsters and withdrew their pistols.

"Were you present at my trial?" Miguel asked in a smooth, low voice. "If I've been found guilty, there must have been a trial. There must have been specific charges. Do you happen to know what they were?"

"Our orders came from the general himself. That's all we need to know."

They needed to know how to kill a man, Miguel thought. Guerrero had work to do if he expected to build his military machine from boys like these. Miguel watched them ready their pistols. The smooth-faced one on the right turned his head and made an attempt to spit in the sand, but his mouth was apparently all but dry. The one on the left wiped a palm on the leg of his camouflage pants. Miguel doubted that either of them would be his murderer, but the man in the center with the lean face might be able to manage it. Miguel decided to die facing the sea.

"Perhaps it would be easier for you if I turned around," he suggested, and he did so.

"Front, back, it makes no difference."

Miguel heard the breech bolts slide back and forth on two of the pistols, and he filled his lungs with a salty breath. One assassin's voice cursed his companions as the words of a well-rehearsed prayer floated across Miguel's mind in time with his heartbeat. The sound of an incoming wave washed across the rude reports of gunfire, and a ball of white heat slammed into his back. Blue water, he thought as he sank to his knees. Blue sky, blue heaven…blue…gray…black.

Chapter 1

This was not the way Paulo Torrez had envisioned his career. De Colores had never had much of an army, but Paulo had seen movies, and true soldiers did not spend day after day patrolling the beach in a rattle-trap jeep. Paulo didn't even get to drive. His cousin Raphael claimed that privilege because he was two years Paulo's senior. Blue sky, endless sea. Everything was calm. Paulo longed for some kind of action.

"Pull over," Paulo demanded as the jeep labored toward the top of a grassy overlook. He spotted a couple of scraggly bushes that would serve his limited modesty.

"What for?" Raphael asked, reluctant to be distracted from his reverie of a young woman he'd met the night before.

"What do you think? You've bounced me in this seat long enough, *hermano*. I'm about to disgrace my uniform."

Raphael grinned as he turned the wheel. "I guess I did promise your mother I would look out for her *niño*, and *niño* is what you are."

"*Bored* is what I am," Paulo said as he climbed down from the jeep. "I would rather clean fish with my father than ride around in this poor excuse for a vehicle from morning till night."

"All right, all right," Raphael grumbled. "I'll let you drive a little while. Just hurry up."

A wide grin split Paulo's boyish face as he spun on his heel and trotted up the hill toward the bushes.

"*Niño,*" Raphael said to himself. "You're too young for this army life." But Paulo had been his shadow ever since Raphael could remember, and Raphael would have had it no other way. If the great battle Colonel Guerrero was always predicting ever came to pass, Raphael would trust no one else in Paulo's foxhole. Personally, Raphael hoped the peace would hold, and that it would not be too late for Paulo to get the education Colonel Hidalgo had promised. Paulo was smart. He'd finished the eighth grade. That was probably why he had deserted his father's fishing boat and followed his cousin into the New People's Army of De Colores. Paulo wanted adventure, but what he really needed, at the tender age of seventeen, was more education.

Something below the bluff had caught Paulo's eye. Raphael slid from the seat as he watched his cousin drop to the ground and peer over the edge. Paulo motioned for silence and signaled Raphael to join him. Raphael snatched up the automatic rifle and was hurrying to join Paulo when he heard the report of gunfire below.

Paulo was struggling to get the pistol out of his holster as Raphael dropped to his side. On the beach below, three men converged upon the body of a fourth. Raphael stilled Paulo's hand with his. "They're out of your range," Raphael whispered.

"But not yours." Paulo nodded at the M-16 in Raphael's grip. "Raphael, I think that was the colonel they shot."

"The colonel?" One of the men knelt in the sand and made a hasty examination of the body.

"It looked like Colonel Hidalgo," Paulo insisted. "Shoot them, Raphael. They've murdered the colonel!"

Raphael looked at his young cousin and saw the outrage in his face. He looked down again. The three were dragging the body across the sand, and he realized that these were men he knew from the barracks. "*Dios*, Paulo, they're...they're on *our* side. I can't just shoot them."

"They shot the colonel!"

Raphael shouldered the rifle and sighted down the barrel. If he pulled the trigger, he wasn't sure what he'd hit. "If he's dead, he's dead, Paulo. We don't know what's going on here."

The three men and the body disappeared into a small cave in the cliff near the water. Paulo cursed his cousin. "I know what I saw. You should have cut the bastards down where they stood, Raphael. What is the matter with you?"

Raphael stared at the entrance to the cave. "We can't go around shooting people just because we carry guns. I have to think about this, Paulo. I have to figure out what's going on. Our own men—"

"There they are! They left him in the cave."

"The tide's coming in," Raphael observed as the three below them moved quickly to quit the scene of their crime. "If the water reaches that cave..."

"The body will be washed away, and we'll have no proof of what we saw." Paulo gestured helplessly. Had the rifle been in his hands, he would have taken a shot at *something*.

"We'll wait until they're gone, and we'll remove the body," Raphael said patiently. "Those three may be renegades."

"Then we should go after them!"

"On the other hand, there may have been another takeover. We must be careful, Paulo."

They moved the jeep to a sheltered spot near a path they knew would take them directly to the beach. It would be a steep climb carrying a corpse, but at least they would not be out in the open. They had to hurry. The tide was already approaching the mouth of the cave.

The body lay facedown in the sand. The cave was dank and filled with the scent of fresh blood. In the dim light Raphael was able to locate the wound in the man's back, while Paulo knelt beside his head and brushed the sand from his face.

"It *is* Colonel Hidalgo." Paulo's awed pronouncement echoed within the close walls. "Why did they do this?"

"I don't know," Raphael said as he cut the rope that bound the colonel's hands. "Help me turn him over."

As they rolled him onto his back, Paulo pulled the colonel's head into his lap. He had seen Colonel Hidalgo at a distance many times, and once, not even very long ago, on the anniversary of the fall of the old regime, the colonel had visited his barracks and shaken his hand. The soldiers had seen more of Colonel Guerrero than they had of Colonel Hidalgo, and many of them were impressed with Guerrero's flashy uniform and tall black boots. His quick temper was also impressive to some, who took it as a sign of power. But Paulo remembered how proud he'd felt when Colonel Hidalgo, whose head now lay so still in his lap, had taken the time to greet him.

"Paulo, I think he's still alive!" Raphael lifted his ear from the colonel's chest and looked at his cousin with wide-eyed hopefulness.

"*¡Dios!* Alive?"

He felt for a pulse on the side of the colonel's neck, taking care not to press too hard. "My own heart is pounding so hard, I can't tell whose is whose, but . . . yes, I think so."

"What can we do?"

"So much blood. Give me your shirt, Paulo."

"Mine?" His camouflage uniform was Paulo's pride and joy. Only those who had special assignments, like patrolling the beaches, were issued uniforms. So far the uniform was all that had made the job worthwhile.

"Your undershirt. I'm not wearing one."

Somewhat relieved, Paulo unbuttoned his shirt.

"Tear it in half. I think the bullet went right through him."

Raphael joined their makeshift canvas belts together and tied them around the colonel's chest to hold the folded pieces of shirt in place over the entrance and exit wounds. Then he lifted the colonel's shoulders, Paulo took his legs, and together they carried him up the side of the mountain. Their years of hauling nets full of fish had prepared them for the job. When they laid him on the back seat of the jeep, he groaned.

"Colonel?" Raphael waited a moment, hoping the colonel would open his eyes. "Bring water, Paulo." No sooner had Raphael uttered the command than the canteen, with its cap dangling open on its chain, appeared at his elbow. "Can you hear me, Colonel Hidalgo? Take a sip of water. Open your eyes and tell us what to do."

There was sand in his mouth, and then there was water. It was the sea. The sea had claimed him. A muffled voice called to him above the water's depths. When he tried to answer, the water filled his mouth again. Struggling with heavy eyelids, he managed to lift them for a brief flash of sunlight, and then every-

thing became murky. Cold. Disjointed. Heavy. Crushing weight on his chest.

"Colonel Hidalgo, please..."

Please what? Please die? Not now. Not yet. Not with the name of... Traitor... Guilty... Cold, cold...

"Open up that canvas, Paulo. Cover him. He's cold."

Traitor... traitor... I'm not a traitor, Paulo.

"Paulo didn't do this to you, sir. Me and Paulo, we saw them. We couldn't stop them. We were... too far away."

The young face was clear, just for a moment. Dark, anxious eyes. Trembling mouth. Kindness, even in the killer.

"You're not dead, sir. Not yet, anyway. You need a doctor."

No doctors. No hospitals. No police... no soldiers.

"Stay with him, Paulo. Keep that tarp over him. We need a place to hide him."

The little landing strip was used only occasionally. It was one of the few spots on the island where fuel was available, albeit at a steep price, and few questions were asked. For a price, security could be relaxed, as well. Raphael remembered a shack that stood at the edge of a sugarcane field adjacent to the landing strip. He thought the colonel might be safe there until Raphael could decide what should be done. He left Paulo in the shack with the wounded man while he went to the village for food and bandages, leaving the jeep well hidden in an overgrown ravine.

As he cut across the field toward the shack, he considered the situation while he surveyed the cane and the stand of trees nearby. He couldn't trust anyone now, and that, more than anything, frightened him. Paulo wanted to shoot first and ask questions later, but Raphael felt the weight of cautious instincts. In addition to buying food and bandages, he had been anxious to hear some bit of conversation that would explain the attempt on Colonel Hidalgo's life. He'd heard nothing.

Paulo stuck his head out the door just as Raphael reached for the latch. "The colonel has regained consciousness," Paulo announced, his eyes bright with the news. "He says the wound is not so bad." Anxious for his cousin to see the improvement for himself, Paulo took the rifle from Raphael's hand and set it against the wall as Raphael closed the door quickly. "The bleeding has stopped," Paulo said, as though he had accomplished it himself.

Raphael cast an apprehensive look at the man who was propped up on the folded tarp. Colonel Hidalgo met Raphael's look with a dark, unemotional stare. Without looking away, Raphael extracted a package from his knapsack before handing it to Paulo. What had this man done? Raphael wondered. In his delirium, the colonel had mumbled something about not being a traitor. Who dared to accuse such an important man? Whose side had Raphael and Paulo taken by rescuing this man from the tide, and against whom were they siding?

"What is your name?" the colonel asked in a low, strained voice.

"Raphael Esperanza." Raphael ripped into the package containing the few medical supplies he had been able to find as he took a step closer. "Corporal Raphael Esperanza."

"You were not with the three who shot me?"

"No. We were on patrol." Raphael cast a quick glance at his cousin, then knelt beside the injured man. "Paulo and me—we were on top of the cliff. We saw them drag you to the cave, but... they were our own men. You had already been shot. We... we didn't know..."

"It's all right," the colonel said. "You acted wisely. Guerrero holds all the cards at the moment."

Paulo stepped closer. "Colonel Guerrero *himself* is responsible for this?"

The colonel closed his eyes and nodded. "I understand he's made himself a general now. He may have caused Castillo's death, too. I don't know."

"Ay," Paulo groaned. "We should have killed them. I knew it!"

"No," Raphael said. "If just one of them had gotten away, they would be combing the island for us by now. As it is, they think the colonel's body has been washed out to sea."

"Where are we?" the colonel asked. His dark eyes probed Raphael's for more than the answer to that question.

"We're near the village of El Gallo. There's a small landing strip." Raphael jerked his chin toward the door. "My uncle's cane field stands out there."

Colonel Hidalgo nodded. "I know the place. It's a good choice, Raphael. There's the possibility of . . . a plane." His features tightened with the strain of his agony.

Raphael reached for the buttons on the man's tattered shirt, then hesitated, asking permission with his eyes. Now that the colonel was conscious, there was his rank to be considered. Hidalgo simply closed his eyes, and Raphael dispatched the buttons quickly. He eased the bloody wad of Paulo's shirt away from the low chest wound.

"Colonel, I must get you to a doctor. All I could find in the village besides some bandages was an antiseptic for the injuries of children." He tossed the cotton aside and examined the wound, from which blood was slowly seeping. Paulo's claim that the bleeding had stopped had been premature. "This wound is serious, too serious for us to—"

"Do the best you can with what you have. With any luck, you will have my undying gratitude."

"What I have—it's not enough," Raphael protested as he examined the small bottle of medicine. When he saw the colonel make a vain attempt to moisten his own lips, he signaled impatiently to Paulo for the canteen.

"It has to be, Raphael. My life is in your hands now."

The very idea chilled Raphael. He held the canteen to the colonel's lips and whispered, "Drink slowly, sir."

"Colonel Guerrero is the wrong man to lead this country," Paulo said quickly. "You must recover from this, Colonel Hidalgo, and we must raise an army, and we must—"

The colonel pushed the canteen away and swallowed as he looked at Paulo. "You must return to your posts. You have already risked too much." He turned to Raphael. "Do what you can to plug up the holes. If you could leave me some food, perhaps a gun ... I might turn hijacker if the right plane—"

"We won't leave you, colonel."

Miguel Hidalgo studied the faces of the two young soldiers who watched him so anxiously. They were just boys. Boys had tried to kill him, and boys had saved his life. All of them should have been working on their fathers' fishing boats or in their uncles' fields. Better yet, they should have been studying in a classroom. But, if Guerrero had his way, they would all carry guns. The boy was right. He had to recover from this.

He took the canteen from Raphael's hand and tipped it to his mouth to slake an overwhelming thirst. Grateful for some measure of relief, he turned his commanding gaze first on Paulo, then on Raphael. "If I am still your colonel, then you will do as I say. Is that clear?" Both nodded. "Good. Then you will do what you can to get me on my feet. If we accomplish that, it will be reasonable to formulate some kind of plan."

The sound of a distant engine cut the conversation short. They listened. They looked at one another, hoping they were all hearing the same sound. A plane!

Paulo crouched behind a pile of old tires as he watched the pilot tend to her plane. She was clearly American. Her hair was tucked into a baseball cap, and her loose-fitting khaki shorts and shirt almost camouflaged her sex. It was obvious that she was no stranger to the island. She knew enough to refuel her plane immediately and be ready to fly. She was alone, she was quite small, and she was perfect, Paulo thought. If she would only go inside the ramshackle gas station and stay there for just a minute or two.

Paulo waited while the woman scrutinized every inch of her twin-engine Cessna. Sweat streamed from his face to his neck as he prepared to take advantage of the first opportunity. Raphael was bandaging the colonel's wounds, and the colonel had agreed to eat what he could of the food Raphael had brought from the village. The colonel was a strong man, Paulo reminded himself. He would survive the trip. There! She'd gone inside. Pistol in hand, Paulo made a dash for the door of the plane.

Miguel slipped his arm into the sleeve of what was left of his shirt as Raphael, kneeling behind him, held the garment up. Miguel took the fact that he could sit up on his own as an encouraging sign. Every move he made cost him precious strength, though, at this point, the show of what strength he had left was for the benefit of the two boys who wanted so desperately to believe in him.

"You and Paulo must return to your posts and tell no one—" urgency glittered in Miguel's eyes as he looked up at Raphael "—*no one* about anything you have seen or done today. If I'm captured, you will not interfere. There are only two of you, Raphael."

"There will be more," the young soldier promised.

"Don't do anything foolish. Please. I'll come back as soon as I'm able. I'll go to El Gallo and I'll get word to you."

Raphael nodded. "I joined in General Castillo's coup last year because I believed he would bring freedom to De Colores," he said. "He promised land, and you talked of a new life for everyone. But Colonel Guerrero is no different from *El Presidente* and the rest of the old regime."

"He's different," Miguel said quietly, thinking what uneasy bedfellows the coup had made of the three of them. "He's more dangerous."

"I want what you've promised us, Colonel Hidalgo. A life without fear. Jobs. Schools for boys like Paulo."

Miguel turned away so that Raphael wouldn't see the amusement in his face. *He* wanted schools for boys like *Raphael*, too. "Teachers are always pushing for schools," he said. "And I'm a teacher. This uniform doesn't fit me."

Raphael eyed the tattered shoulder of the colonel's shirt, where the symbols of his rank had been ripped away. "You don't need the uniform, Colonel Hidalgo. Just come back and lead us. We'll follow you."

The boy's faith in him made him shudder inwardly. Through the triumvirate, Miguel had unwittingly helped Guerrero gain unlimited access to power. What if he couldn't come back? What would happen to these boys and others like them? The answers crowded into his mind along with the pain, and all of it made his head swim. "Take a look outside," he said gruffly. "See what's taking that cousin of yours so long."

Ronnie Harper felt uneasy. There was only one small window in the place, and the quarters were too close for comfort. She'd contracted to fly into this hornet's nest to help some people escape, and the sooner she could take on her passengers and hightail it out of here, the better she'd like it.

From a dark corner of the building a radio was blasting a mixture of static and calypso music. Ronnie handed a roll of bills to the man behind the pile of crates that made up the counter in this so-called gas station. She had included the mandatory "tip" as payment for no questions asked, then informed the little man that she'd brought Red Cross supplies. He smiled as he examined the American currency. As long as the money was good, he obviously didn't care what she'd brought.

"I'll move my plane to the other side of the strip," she told him in Spanish. "I won't be here more than a few days." I hope, she added to herself.

The dark-haired man shrugged as he pocketed Ronnie's money. When the music was interrupted, he wiped his hand on his oil-stained T-shirt and turned the radio up. The announcement of an emergency bulletin caught Ronnie's attention, and she concentrated on separating the Spanish from the static and making sense of the message.

"Sad duty to report... Colonel Miguel Hidalgo's death... assassinated by a rebel faction... state of emergency..."

"Ay," the dark-haired man groaned.

Damn, Ronnie thought. The hornet's nest had become a snake pit. *"Es una verguenza,"* she sympathized. And it certainly *was* a shame. Her written permission to fly supplies in from the Red Cross came from Hidalgo. Of course, she had no permission to fly her passengers out, which was one of her reasons for choosing this particular airstrip—that and its proximity to El Gallo.

"Yes, it is a shame," the man agreed. "Now we have only... the one."

Ronnie knew little about the three men who had overthrown the island's old regime, but "the one" inspired a fearful tone even in this man's voice. Two down and one to go. It sounded as though dictators were dropping like flies. She decided to make herself as inconspicuous as possible while she waited in El Gallo for her passengers to show up. Meanwhile, she did have supplies to deliver to the Red Cross office in the capital city, La Primavera.

"I don't suppose you have a phone?" she asked. The man shook his head. "I'll move my plane, then."

Wearily, Ronnie walked outside and climbed into the cockpit. She'd logged a lot of flight time in the past couple of days, and she was glad for the delay in one respect—she could get some rest. Then she heard a deadly click behind her head, and cold metal rested against her warm neck. The thought of rest flew out the window.

"Don't turn around, *señorita*. Take this plane to the end of the runway. Do as I say, and I promise not to hurt you."

"Which end?" Ronnie asked calmly.

"The east end. Near that shack."

Ronnie did as she was told. She didn't need to turn around. She could tell by his voice that the man who held the gun to her head was young and scared, a dangerous combination. She turned her head slightly and watched two men emerge from the shack. They were soldiers. The young, lanky one wore camouflage fatigues, and the older man was dressed in tattered khakis. Ronnie's attention was drawn to the latter, the trim, broad-shouldered man, who had apparently been injured. He held his hand tightly over his left side, and he refused the young soldier's assistance as they walked quickly toward the plane. When the injured man stumbled, the man with the gun started a bit, but the young soldier on the ground lent a steadying hand. The door to the aircraft was flung open, and Ronnie sat quietly, listening as the wounded man struggled to climb aboard.

"Move back, Paulo," a rich, deep voice said. "Let's let our pilot turn around. Very slowly, please."

Ronnie turned to face a man who looked as haggard as he did handsome, sitting in the back seat between two teenage boys who were dressed up as soldiers. The boys were scared, but the man appeared to be calm. His dark eyes betrayed fatigue, but no emotion.

"Give me your pistol," he told the man who had accompanied him to the plane. The young soldier slid the clip from the butt of the gun and satisfied himself that the weapon was fully loaded before handing it over.

Ronnie willed her voice to sound confident as she eyed each man's face. "What's going on?" she asked quietly.

"You're taking me for a ride," the injured man said.

"Where?"

"We'll discuss that as soon as we're in the air."

"I think I should go with you," the man who'd commandeered the plane said. "You might—"

The wounded man shook his head. "I've given your cousin my orders. You are to follow them to the letter."

"But I can't leave the island just yet," Ronnie blurted. With three pairs of dark eyes and the black muzzles of two pistols staring her in the face, she knew she was in no position to lodge an effective protest. "I, um . . . I have papers signed by Colonel Hidalgo himself," she explained. "Permission to deliver Red Cross supplies. If I could just . . ."

The injured man managed a crooked smile. "I'm afraid those papers will no longer do you any good, *señorita*."

"Well, there's something else. I have another very important job to do, and if you could just wait a couple of days—"

"I don't have a couple of days." The older man motioned the other two toward the door, but his attention did not waver from Ronnie. "Go on, now." The two young soldiers obeyed immediately. "And be careful," their leader told them as they jumped down from the plane.

"Get this crate in the air," the man demanded in slightly accented English.

"You don't look like you're in very good shape to me," Ronnie returned. "What if you—"

"I won't," he assured her smoothly. "And unless you turn around in your seat and fly this plane, you may find yourself in poor shape, as well. I believe I could handle this machine myself."

Ronnie assessed the dark look in his eyes and the equally black hole in the muzzle of the gun. Then she turned her attention to the controls.

Chapter 2

Ronnie retracted the landing gear and prayed that the man with the gun would pass out soon as she watched the nose of her plane point toward blue sky. She knew he couldn't hold out long. He was already half dead. Of course, she didn't want him to go all the way, but if he would just lose consciousness and drop that gun, she would feel a lot better. Gripping the wheel, she eased the nose down for a normal climb. The controls were in her hands, but the gun in his made her uneasy. She wanted to hear it fall to the floor and know that her passenger was out cold. When he climbed into the seat beside her, her hopes slipped a notch. But glancing to the side, she saw the pallor in his face and they rose again.

"You will take me to Florida," he said. His voice was strong, but his exhaustion could not be masked.

"That's ridiculous. What would I do with you? You can't expect to get past customs."

"I'm sure you can find a discreet place to land this plane so that I won't have to deal with that problem."

Ronnie glanced down at the gun, which was no longer pointed directly at her. He held it loosely, almost as though he'd forgotten about it. "Let me take you to Arco Iris. You know, that little island west of here. It's Mexican territory. You should be safe there."

"I *should* be safe in De Colores," he said. "I'm not, which means I'm not safe anywhere."

"I didn't know there was any fighting going on there." Ronnie waited for an explanation of his situation, but he studied the gauges and offered no comment. "Arco Iris is closer," she continued. "I have passengers waiting in De Colores—or, at least, they will be. They're depending on me. I could just drop you off on Arco Iris and go—"

"We're going to Florida." Miguel knew he needed help, and he knew someone in Florida who might help him. After all, McQuade owed him a favor after Miguel had helped the private investigator and his friend, Mikal Romanov, get a group of hostages safely off the island and out of Guerrero's reach. "Your other passengers can wait a couple of days."

"If I'm not there when I'm supposed to be, they could be in as much trouble as you are." Ronnie cast a pointed look at the man's wounded side. "Who's after you, anyway?"

"My partner, I guess."

"Nice guy." Her gaze traveled from his blood-stained shirt to his dark eyes. "I heard about Hidalgo's assassination. Were you with him?"

Miguel lifted the corner of his mouth in an attempt to smile. "You have my signature on your papers but we have never met."

"Miguel Hidalgo's signature is on my papers, and he's dead," Ronnie insisted. She had gained the altitude she wanted and was leveling off smoothly. "I heard it on the radio."

"The news of my death came a bit prematurely."

Her eyes widened. "You're *Hidalgo*?"

She was an American, he told himself, with an American conscience—that wonderful aversion to kicking a man when he's down. She delivered Red Cross supplies. She was concerned about the passengers she'd left behind, who were probably also on Guerrero's hit list.

He decided to trust her. He knew he had no choice. "I regret having to introduce myself to you with a .45 in my hand, Miss Harper."

"I don't think you regret it half as much as I do, colonel. It takes all the fun out of flying."

He smiled indulgently. "And what would you do if I put the gun away?"

She glanced away from him. "Three people are depending on me to fly them off that island. I'd go back for them."

"I thought you would."

"Colonel—"

"I'm no longer a colonel, Miss Harper. As you can see, they stripped me of that burden prior to my execution."

"Pretty sorry excuse for an execution, if you ask me," Ronnie grumbled. His weakened condition was evident even in the sound of his quick laugh. Ronnie found herself wondering how much blood he'd lost and wishing she had some way of replenishing it right there on the plane.

"I can't be held responsible for that. Guerrero's in charge of military training." He dropped his head back against the seat and sighed. The sun's brightness hurt his eyes, and he wanted to shut it out somehow. "The three who were chosen for the job of shooting me are obviously in need of more practice. Would you have me offer them my back again? Perhaps they can get it right the second time."

"No, of course not. If your boys had just explained what was going on, I probably could have gotten everybody out safely."

"There was no time. Believe me, Miss Harper, there was no . . ." Miguel jerked his head up. He'd nearly fallen asleep. Or passed out—he wasn't sure which. "Those two boys would have been killed, too, simply for helping me," he said quickly. "It isn't that my life is more valuable than anyone else's. But I have to try to stop Guerrero."

"In the shape you're in, you'd have trouble stopping a mosquito." She raised an eyebrow in his direction. "And any blood sucked out of you at this point would probably push you beyond the brink."

"Such blunt words from such a sweet face," he muttered, studying the gauges again. He'd lied when he'd said he could fly the plane himself, but he knew something about the instruments, and he could tell that they were on course. He wanted her to believe that, if need be, he could handle the craft as skillfully as she did.

"Sweet?" Ronnie laughed uneasily. Kids were sweet. Baby faces were sweet. He looked at her and probably saw both. And he was...classy, she decided. His clothes were tattered, his face drawn with pain, and he was a fugitive from his own government. Yet he bore himself with imperturbable dignity. *And* he was about as handsome as any man Ronnie had ever met.

"Kind," he amended quietly. "You have a kind face. I believe, Miss Harper, that if I hadn't the strength to fight off a mosquito, you would take it upon yourself to chase it away."

She added the word *charming* to her mental assessment, and she had to remind herself that this classy, dignified, handsome, charming man was pointing a gun at her. Well, *almost* at her. She reached behind her seat and found the lunch she'd packed for herself that morning before taking off from Arco Iris. She saw that his hand tightened around the grip of the gun. Matching bracelets of raw skin suggested that his wrists had recently been bound.

"I don't carry a gun, Colonel—*Mr.* Hidalgo. But I do carry—" she extracted a bottle from the paper bag "—orange juice. You'd better drink all you can."

When he hesitated, eyeing the screw cap, she shook the contents, opened the bottle and offered it again. He took it with his free hand. "Miguel," he corrected as he raised the bottle to his mouth. The juice was not cold, but it was wet, and it tasted good. His look was grateful as he repeated, "My name is Miguel."

She smiled, and her azure eyes glowed softly. "I'm not afraid of you any more, Miguel. I really don't think you'd shoot me."

"Please don't put me to the test, Miss Harper."

No, she wouldn't. She wanted to persist in her belief without conducting any tests. "Ronnie," she said quietly.

"Ronnie," he repeated.

She offered him a sandwich, and he accepted it hoping he could quell the light-headedness he felt, but he could only eat a few bites. He held the gun with one hand and his wounded side with the other and struggled to remain conscious. There were moments when the instrument panel became blurry, and he'd blink several times in an effort to refocus. His chest throbbed, his back burned, and he took shallow breaths, hoping to disturb the holes in his body as little as possible. He knew he was losing the battle. God help him, he couldn't pass out.

"Miguel." Her voice seemed distant. He concentrated his energy on looking at her, keeping his head up and his eyes open. "I'm taking you to the Keys," she said. "To my house. It's in an isolated spot. You'll be safe there."

"Good," he managed to say, though the word sounded like a grunt. In an attempt to keep his act from falling apart, he tried again. "That's good."

"Let me have the gun now."

It was a gentle order. A soft command. He felt the pistol slide from his fingers, and he couldn't close his hand. It didn't matter, he thought as he rested his head against the back of the seat. He could never have shed her blood, and she knew it. The act was over.

Ronnie removed the ammunition clip from the pistol and dropped it in the paper bag, along with the remainder of her lunch. The pistol itself she stowed in the pocket of her jacket. She could do anything she wanted with this man now. He was completely helpless. She could open the door and shove him into the sea if she wanted to. After all, he was a hijacker. He'd held a gun on her. He'd messed up an important job.

His head lolled to one side, and she reached quickly for the hand that lay limp on his thigh. His pulse was not strong, but it was steady. He needed a doctor. He needed to be in a hospital. She'd promised to take him to her house, but there was no doctor on the island she lived on. There was Becky Gordon, her neighbor, but Becky was a retired nurse, not a doctor.

There was another promise she had to keep, and that was the one she'd made to Elizabeth Donnelly. Elizabeth had hired a man named McQuade, who was some kind of high-priced troubleshooter, to help her get her baby son out of De Colores. Elizabeth and McQuade were going to hire a fishing boat to take them to the island, and Ronnie was to meet them in El

Gallo and fly them out. She wasn't sure how long it would take them to get there or to find the child, but her instructions had been to leave word at the cantina and to wait for a message from McQuade. They had paid her well, but, more than that, she had come to think of the beautiful woman as a friend, and Ronnie Harper never deserted her friends.

They wouldn't have reached the island yet. Ronnie figured she had a little time. She didn't know much about the politics in De Colores other than that it had been ruled by a three-man junta until just recently. The death of one of those men and the attempted murder of another within a few days' time seemed a little too convenient for the third. She decided she had time to get help for this man.

Miguel's seat seemed to roll beneath him. His first thought was of the sea, but the roar of the plane's engines crowded that thought from his mind as he fought with heavy eyelids. When he succeeded in lifting them, the light speared his eyes. He covered them quickly with his hand and rubbed them with his fingertips and his thumb.

"How are you feeling?"

It was the soft, melodic voice of a woman. He lowered his hand slowly and opened his eyes, letting them adjust to the light. Ronnie, he remembered. The American woman. She'd taken off her baseball cap, and her reddish-blond hair fell past her shoulders. It looked as soft as her voice sounded.

"A little seasick," he mumbled.

"We've run into some low-level turbulence. Nothing major." She hadn't radioed ahead for clearance yet, but she'd decided on a new flight plan. She had an emergency on her hands. "I'm going to take you to a hospital, Miguel. You need medical attention."

As he struggled to sit up, he remembered that he was unarmed. As he'd lost consciousness, she'd taken his gun. She smiled at him, but not, as he might have expected, in triumph. It was a reassuring smile. She intended to help him, but she had her own ideas about the best way to do that.

"If you take me to a hospital, I may very well be sent back to De Colores," he told her, "where I would be killed."

"But not if you tell them what happened. You can ask for political asylum."

"Guerrero has declared that I'm a traitor. I'm told there was even a trial of some sort. He'll demand extradition."

"But, Miguel, surely the United States government wouldn't turn you over to Guerrero after what he's done to you."

"I can't take that chance." It took a great deal of effort simply to shift in his seat so that he could observe the expression on her face. "Guerrero thinks I'm dead. I was left in a cave on the beach, and the incoming tide would have washed me away if Raphael and Paulo hadn't come along when they did."

Ronnie stared at him for a moment. "You do know that without the proper medical attention, you might die anyway."

"Given a choice," he said evenly, "that is the chance I would prefer to take. Even if I am granted asylum, Guerrero has many contacts. I would be dead before the week was out."

"My God," Ronnie said. "What am I going to do?"

"You said... you would take me to your house. I would try very hard... not to die in your bed." He tried to smile, but he wasn't sure his face was cooperating. His vision was cloudy.

"Don't even suggest it. Where would I..." She turned to him and scowled. "Don't you pass out on me again! Miguel, is there anyone I could notify?"

He closed his eyes and rolled his head back and forth on the back of the seat. "I have no family. Except... my father. Lives in Geneva. His name... Roderigo."

It was after sundown when Ronnie landed her plane on the strip near her beach house. She had radioed Marathon Airport that she was having engine trouble and was making an emergency landing, which meant that she would have to pay a customs official overtime to come out and clear her. She would have time to get Miguel into the house and invent some kind of engine trouble.

The plane's touchdown roused Miguel. He lifted his head and peered out the side window, trying to make sense of the shadows in the twilight. Water and trees seemed to whiz by the window in shades of gray. He turned to Ronnie, his face a reflection of his muddled mind.

"It's all right," she said, sparing him only a quick glance. "This is where I live. Ordinarily I use Marathon Airport, but I told them I had to make an emergency landing." She knew this strip of ground, but she knew the low light could play tricks on a pilot's eyes. "We'll get you into the house before the agent comes. Can you walk?"

"What agent?"

"Customs," she said as easily as she might have said mail carrier. "I've been outside the country. I have to get clearance." She shut the engines down and turned to him. "Don't worry. You'll be safe in the house. If we can get you there, that is."

He sighed. "I can walk."

"I'll have to rig up something to make it look like I really had engine trouble, and . . . I do have to get you some help, Miguel."

"Just get me some bandages," he said wearily, "and some kind of—"

"I have a friend who's a nurse. I trust her."

"I'm supposed to trust her because *you* trust her?"

Ronnie grabbed her jacket and the paper bag. "You don't have any choice," she informed him over her shoulder as she opened the door. "I've got the gun now."

Miguel leaned heavily on Ronnie's shoulders as they made their way to her front door. She tossed her jacket and lunch bag on a chair and turned a light on. The only bed in the house was at the top of a flight of narrow steps in the little garret bedroom. Miguel made heavy use of the handrail and Ronnie's surprisingly

plentiful strength in getting up the stairs. In near
darkness she did her best to ease him down to the bed,
but when his legs finally buckled and he collapsed, she
went down with him. Her arm was trapped under his
back, and when she tried to lever herself away from
him, he groaned and shoved her hand away. Down she
went again.

Her hand was wet, and her heart was pounding. His
chest heaved beneath her head as he struggled to gain
control. A terrible shudder rippled through his body,
and he rolled his head to the side, where she lay very
still. She listened to the air rush in and out as his
panting became shallower, and she knew he was
fighting off a blackout.

"I'm sorry," she whispered, now frightened for him
rather than of him. "I made it start bleeding again."

"No... not you. The walk..."

His shirt was damp with sweat. When he turned his
head more, his chin rested against her forehead. His
face was wet, too. She stopped trying to pull away and
simply let her arm be around him, let her head rest
against him and let her body absorb his trembling. "I
was carrying medical supplies for the Red Cross," she
said quietly. "They're still on the plane. Becky will be
able to fix you up."

"You can... *you* can take care of me yourself."

Ronnie eased herself away from him and helped him
get his legs on the bed. Then she turned the switch on
a table lamp. Miguel put his hand over his eyes, shun-
ning the light.

"I can't," she said finally. "I don't know how." She went into the tiny bathroom at the other end of the garret and took two clean bath towels from a shelf above the commode. Returning to his side, she sat on the edge of the bed and unbuttoned his shirt as she talked. "Listen, you're not in a hospital *yet*, so just be grateful for small favors. But you need help. *I* need help. I'm not sure I even want to look at this."

She drew the shirt back from his chest. The thick pad of gauze and the strips of bandaging holding it in place were red with the spreading evidence of more bleeding. Ronnie lifted her eyes slowly from the wound to Miguel's face. His eyes were glazed with pain.

"It looks awful."

"You haven't seen anything yet, Miss Harper. And there's another one in back just like it."

"That must be a good sign." She glanced down and then up again. "The bullet must have gone right through you."

"I find that encouraging." He realized that his throat was as dry as the remark.

"But there's no telling what it might have ripped through along the way." She leaned across him to open the little window above the brass headboard. The smell of his blood was making her head spin.

A request for water had been on the tip of his tongue, but when the front of her loose-fitting khaki shirt drooped close to his face and one white button brushed the tip of his nose, the words vanished. Beneath the shirt, smooth, honey-toned skin disappeared into a vee of unadorned white cotton. From his vantage point the cleft between her breasts looked like an arch through which a man might pass on his way to heaven. He wondered whether this was a sign that he was on his way.

"There, that's much better." Ronnie sat back quickly and caught his wistful smile. Her hand flew to her chest, pressing her shirt tightly, and she felt her face grow warm despite the cool breeze from the window.

"Thank you," he said in a voice as mellow as the look in his eyes had become.

"I have to get back to the plane before they come." She glanced around nervously, saw the towels and snatched them up. "I'd better get some sterile supplies off the plane before I take this bandage off. Was this stuff sterile?"

He lifted one corner of his mouth. "I forgot to ask."

"Can you lift up a little?" She tucked one towel under his back and laid the other on top. "Hold this." When he didn't move, she took his hand and pressed it against the towel. "I think if you could apply some pressure here, it might help."

He nodded. "How long will you be gone?"

Ronnie studied his face. His dark eyes glittered, and his jaw was set. Black hair tumbled over his forehead, which glistened in the lamplight with a fine sheen of perspiration. He knew more about the extent of his injuries than she did. He had to. He could feel the pain. His question was the first hint that he might be afraid of what he knew.

"I've got to make it look like we had an oil leak or something. Most of the agents know who I am. I won't have any problem with clearance. Then I'm going to get you some help."

"Please don't involve anyone else."

"Listen, mister." She cast a look at the pitched ceiling and inhaled deeply. Then she expelled a long, slow sigh as she looked at him again. "I'd have a heck of a time coming up with a good explanation for your corpse."

"I'm not dead yet," he pointed out. "It must not be very serious."

"Yeah, right," she tossed back as she pressed her small hand over his. "Hold this tight, okay?"

"May I . . . have some water?"

She saw a flash of fear in his eyes, and her breath caught in her chest. "Of course." She moved quickly, coming back from the bathroom with a glass of water and a damp washcloth. He started to raise himself on his elbow, but she was there before he'd expended much energy. She slid her arm beneath him and supported his head on her shoulder while she held the glass to his lips. "Slowly," she warned when she saw how thirsty he was. "I don't know why, but they always say that when people get hurt."

"Who says that?" he asked when she lowered the glass.

"People in movies." She smiled at him. "I like to go to movies. Especially movies about the past, with lots of gorgeous costumes.'' She lifted the glass again. ''More?''

He turned his head and grunted, which she interpreted as a decline of the offer. ''If this were a movie, you would take out your mother's embroidery basket and repair whatever the bullet ripped through,'' he told her.

Carefully she withdrew her support, and he settled his head back on her pillow. ''If this were a movie, your shirt would be covered with catsup instead of blood,'' she countered as she daubed the cool cloth over his forehead. ''Besides, my mother died long before she had a chance to teach me anything about sewing, so you're just going to have to trust my friend Becky.''

She avoided his eyes as she swabbed the sweat from his neck. His eyes never left her face. She felt their heat, and when she stood up and took a step back, she was reminded of the sensation she had stepping back from stoking a fire. She cleared her throat. ''I'd better hurry.''

''Is that catsup on your shirt, or is it more of my blood?''

She glanced down at the red stain. ''Oh, gosh, I'd better check the seats out there, too.'' She pulled the closet door open and snatched another shirt off a hanger. Her fingers froze on the top button of the shirt she wore, and she glanced furtively to see whether he'd noticed the reflex. His attention was fixed on the bathroom door.

"Do you need . . . anything else?" she asked as she edged toward the stairs.

"No," he said quietly. And as she started down the steps he called to her. "Don't worry, my little angel of mercy," he said. "If something goes wrong, I won't forget to tell them that you agreed to all this at gunpoint."

"Nothing's going to go wrong," she promised. And then she was gone.

Ronnie had a lot to do and not much time to get it done. Buttoning her clean shirt with one hand, she used the other to stuff her stained shirt under the lid of the compact washer in the kitchen, spray cleaning fluid on a rag and take a flashlight from the cupboard. With her buttons in order, she hurried back to her plane.

The yellow beam from the flashlight revealed blood smeared like fingerpaint over the tan vinyl seats, both front and back. Ronnie cleaned them thoroughly before turning to the motor. She drained the oil from the left engine, dribbled it around generously to fake an oil leak and set up a repair scene for the benefit of the driver of the boat that was just putting in at her dock. She proceeded to bewail her troubles to the customs agent as she explained that she'd dropped two passengers off in Arco Iris and headed for De Colores. She showed him she'd returned with all the cargo she had intended to deliver to the Red Cross office in De Colores.

"Didn't they want it?" the agent asked.

"They're all in a tizzy down there." Ronnie shut the cargo bay and opened the side door, gesturing for the agent to have a look inside. "Some colonel got himself assassinated, and they wouldn't clear my plane. I was lucky they let me refuel and come home."

"Guess so." The sandy-haired young man took a seat and filled out his forms under the plane's interior light. "Too bad about your leakage problem. How long since you had your gaskets checked?"

"It isn't a gasket," she said as she braced her hand on the doorway. "It might be the fuel-pump seal. I'll take care of it tomorrow."

He signed his name with a flourish and handed her a copy of her customs clearance with a smile. "Long day, huh?"

"It's been a killer," she admitted. "Or damn near."

Ronnie had lived on the little key with no name for as long as she could remember, and Becky Gordon had always owned the small cottage with the red roof, the one Ronnie could see from her kitchen window. There was a time when Becky only spent summers there, but that was long ago. Ronnie sometimes thought Becky had retired from nursing just to help Ronnie survive adolescence, which hadn't been an easy time for a girl living with a house full of men. Her father hadn't known quite what to do with her until he had hit upon the idea that she wasn't really that much different from her two older brothers, and had begun to treat her as such. When she'd needed to know more about what it meant to be female, Becky was there to help her.

Ronnie had never needed Becky's help more than she needed it now, and once again she found herself knocking on Becky's door with a head full of questions. Her heart pounded, and she knew she was just as fearful of the answers as she had been when she was twelve years old. Something was terribly wrong. Blood scared her, and she'd never seen so much blood.

A tall, slender woman with short gray hair appeared at the door in her bathrobe. Her frown disappeared as she raised her brow in amazement. "Back so soon? I thought you said you'd be down in the islands for a week or more."

Ronnie backed the woman inside and closed the door. "I need your help, Becky. I've got a friend. He's . . . he's been hurt really bad."

Becky was a nurse by nature as well as by profession. Retirement hadn't modified her reaction to the news that someone was hurt. Her scuffs flapped against her heels as she headed for the bedroom untying the sash of her robe. Her questions trailed behind her. "Where is he, honey?"

"At my house."

"What happened?"

"Somebody shot him."

Becky tossed her robe on the bed and turned back to the young woman who stood in the doorway. "Somebody *shot* him?"

"Yes, Becky, he's been shot. Please hurry." Ronnie spotted a pair of Becky's shoes under a chair, and she lunged for them. "He was shot in the back...sort of to one side...came out the front, I guess. There's just so much blood, and I don't know—"

Becky tied a wraparound skirt over her short night-gown and took the shoes Ronnie handed her. "Is he conscious?"

"Most of the time." Ronnie swept Becky's favorite white cardigan off the chair and held it up for her.

"What we need to do is get him to an emergency room. Have you called—"

"I can't, Becky." Her eyes met the older woman's over the sweater's shawl collar. "He's in trouble."

If Ronnie was willing to help him, Becky was, too. And if Ronnie was willing to protect him, Becky didn't have to ask whether the trouble was of his own making. "I don't have much to work with," Becky said regretfully. "I've got my old Africa bag, but it's been a long time since—"

"I'll get it," Ronnie said as she turned toward the closet. She'd always loved Becky's stories of the time she'd spent nursing in the missionary outposts in Africa. The medical bag was kept on a high shelf in the closet, still just beyond Ronnie's grasp.

Becky reached over Ronnie's head and took the bag down. "But I don't have any kind of antiseptic, no sterile bandages, nothing for...wait a minute." She went to the medicine cabinet in the bathroom, took a couple of bottles down and dropped them into the bag. "They don't do me much good, anyway," she muttered.

"I've got a bunch of stuff on the plane," Ronnie called out. "Stuff the Red Cross ordered."

Becky emerged from the bathroom. "This man had better not be some drug runner, missy."

"He's not. I swear." She took Becky's elbow and scooted her along. "I'll tell you everything I know, but we've got to hurry. I think he's pretty bad off."

The sound of voices swirled around the fringe of Miguel's elusive consciousness. When he became aware that the voices were somewhere in the house, he tried to sit up, but he struggled in vain. He gave up, lay still and watched the top of the steps. A gray head appeared first, a woman carrying a black bag. A doctor? God, he needed a doctor. He'd almost be grateful, even if it meant the young woman had betrayed him.

"I'm here to try to help you," the woman said as she approached the bedside. "Miguel, isn't it? Ronnie tells me your name is Miguel."

"Yes," he managed to say over a dry tongue. He was still clutching the towel against his side as Ronnie had instructed. "Miguel."

"I'm not a physician, Miguel." The woman set her bag on the table near the bed and sat down in a straight-backed chair that had appeared near her hand. When she was seated, he saw Ronnie standing behind her. "I want you to understand that. I am a nurse practitioner, long retired. You'd be much better off if you'd let us send for a doctor."

"You know my situation?"

"Ronnie tells me you have some powerful enemies." Becky opened her bag as she spoke.

"It's important that I return to De Colores. I can't
afford the complications that doctors and hospitals
might cause."

Becky moved Miguel's hand and took the towel
away. "We're going to need those supplies, Ronnie,"
she said over her shoulder. "Bring in everything
you've got, and let's hope we can put together the
right combination."

Returning with a large plastic garbage bag full of
packages, Ronnie overheard Becky's use of a word
that meant more trouble. "Surgery?" she croaked as
she let the bag slide to the floor. She noticed a pile of
bloody bandages lying on a newspaper beside the bed.
"You can't be serious."

Becky turned from her patient, eyed the bag and
then looked up at Ronnie. "I was just explaining to
Miguel that I did all kinds of surgery when I was out
in the bush. Lots of times when it needed to be done,
there was no one else to do it. Sort of like now."

"Can't you just sew him up?"

"Essentially, yes, but this man is in a lot of pain,
and there's a lot of blood here." Ronnie went around
to the opposite side of the bed, and Becky turned to
Miguel. "I think the bullet might have nicked the
bowel, which means that has to be sewn up, too. I
haven't done anything like that in a long time."

"At least you've done it," Miguel said in a tight
voice. "My friend here tells me she knows nothing
about sewing." He looked at Ronnie and offered a

thin smile. She read the message in his eyes. He needed a friend, and she was all he had.

"I've got some more bad news," Becky continued. "We don't have access to any controlled drugs, and I can tell you right now, there aren't any in that Red Cross shipment. Which means no painkillers and no anesthetic. All I have is what I take for arthritis, which might give you some relief after we're done." Miguel closed his eyes and gave a nod of understanding.

Ronnie braced herself on both arms and leaned closer to him. "This would be a good time for you to stop fighting it and just pass out."

Becky examined her own gnarled fist. "I used this once. In those days I packed quite a wallop." She acknowledged Miguel's attempt to smile, and then she had another idea. "Ronnie, don't you keep some whiskey around for your dad?"

"I think there's some." She got to her feet quickly. "I don't know how much."

"How much would it take for you to reach the feeling-no-pain stage, Miguel?" Becky asked.

He groaned. "At this point, just the smell."

"Did you see anything in that bag labeled sterile bandages?"

Becky's question stopped Ronnie before she reached the stairs. "Yeah, lots of it."

"Toss me a package of it."

Miguel welcomed the whiskey as a thirst-quencher as much as anything else. It didn't take much to separate him from what little grip he had left on his sense of reality. With his head pillowed on Ronnie's shoulder, he began to drift; and he decided that the shoulder of this angel was a pleasant conveyance for drifting. She fed him little sips, and he tried to ignore the woman who had removed his shirt and was swabbing his side with something cool.

"Your eyes are the color of the sea," he told his angel. His tongue was thick, and he took pains to enunciate each word slowly so that she would understand. "Both green and blue. More green with indignation. Blue steals across them softly with your compassion."

Ronnie smiled. The whiskey was working. The man was definitely hallucinating.

"You've got yourself a smooth talker there, missy."

Ronnie glanced up at Becky, who was working on Miguel's belt buckle. "You're not going to take his pants off, too."

"They're filthy," Becky muttered. "When you've seen as many naked men as I have, they all start looking pretty much alike."

"Becky, for heaven's sake," Ronnie whispered.

"And we'll have to tie his hands to the bed. Probably his legs, too. We can't have him—"

"No." At the sound of the word, Ronnie looked down, and Miguel searched through the encroaching haze for the blue in her eyes. He remembered his last walk on the beach. The rope that bound him had rubbed his wrists raw. "You won't tie my hands."

"Just to keep you from thrashing about, you understand. You might think you can stand the pain, young man, but this could be one heck of a . . ."

Ronnie tuned out Becky's warnings and allowed Miguel to draw her into the depths of his dark eyes. Within a few short hours Ronnie had become his ally. He was being stripped of all his clothes before two women he didn't know, and in a moment one of them would fillet his flesh and lace it up again. All he asked was to be spared the indignity of being trussed like an animal.

"There'll be no need to tie his hands," she told Becky. "I'll hold them."

Chapter 3

Miguel's thick, dark eyelashes were hovering at half-mast, but his eloquent way with words, even when the words were slurred, impressed Ronnie. He praised her hair, her good sense, her smile and her skill as a pilot. He could have almost convinced her that she had relatives on Mount Olympus had she not been determined to put every beautiful word he said in perspective with the situation at hand. The man was at her mercy as he lay there bleeding all over her bed while she poured whiskey down his throat. Still, she enjoyed the words. Never before had so many pretty ones been directed her way.

"Forgive me for frightening you with the gun," he said.

"I wasn't scared." She had helped him turn on his side, and she sat beside him on the bed with her back to Becky's preparations. Miguel was covered from the waist down with a clean sheet, and Becky had boiled her instruments while Ronnie rigged a mechanic's trouble light over the bed.

Miguel offered a sleepy smile. "Not even at first? Tell me the truth."

"That young soldier scared me when he popped up in the back seat. I'll have to admit that."

"But I didn't?"

"What would you have done if I'd refused to follow your orders?" she asked, half teasing.

His eyes slid closed, and he sighed. "I don't know."

"Are you ready?" Becky asked.

The ominous question brought Miguel fully awake. He fixed his gaze on the place where the pitched roof met the wall. "Go ahead."

His whole body tensed with the initial shock of another steel-tipped assault. His head came up off the pillow, but he held fast to his focus on the wall. The muscles in Ronnie's stomach tightened as she read the pain in his face. She laid her hand on his shoulder. As the seconds ticked by, he began to tremble. Beads of perspiration shone brightly on his tanned face.

"Try to relax, Miguel," Becky said. "Try not to move at all."

Ronnie started to look over her shoulder.

"Don't!" All the fire and fear in his black eyes met hers. "Don't . . . watch her . . . carve me up!"

Ronnie touched his forehead, let her fingers slide into his damp hair and gently pushed his head back against the pillow. "I won't," she promised.

He closed his eyes and worked to control his breathing. "Talk to me, angel." Looking up again, he pleaded quietly, "Talk to me."

Distract him, he meant. Dear Lord, how could she? What could she say? She leaned closer, curling around him to shield his face from Becky's work. "The whiskey didn't help much, did it?" she sympathized as she combed his thick, black hair back from his face. "The first time in my life I've ever tried to get a man drunk, and he refuses to cooperate."

"Next time," he grunted. "But give me... better cause."

"This cause is a good one, Miguel. Becky's going to fix you up, just like new. Hold on, now." She stroked his face, trying to smooth away the strain. "It'll be over soon. You're doing fine. You're doing just fine." She caressed his shoulder, kneading the hard ridge of muscle.

"Liar," he gasped, and he snatched her hand and crushed it in his.

"No, no, I've never seen anyone... so strong..." His head came up off the pillow again, and she wasn't sure whether the groan she heard was his or her own. "Oh, dear God," she whispered as she scooted her knees beneath his head and pulled his face against her belly.

"This part's going to hurt," Becky muttered.

This part? Ronnie braced herself for the pain as Miguel's free arm encircled her hips. His other arm was trapped beneath his body, but he groped for a second handhold and found her ankle. Ronnie's breath caught in her throat. His groans were muffled in her lap until he finally slipped into blessed unconsciousness.

"Is he out finally? Thank God," Becky said.

"Thank God." Ronnie sighed, feeling physically relieved. She continued to hold him, shutting out the smell of sweat and blood as she stroked his hair.

The Red Cross was the unwitting supplier of tetanus serum and antibiotics, both of which Becky injected into her patient. She would have traded the gross of thermometers for a couple of pints of blood and the wherewithal to match and transfuse it. As she taped his bandages in place, she gave Miguel a silent order to step up the manufacture of his own blood. Finally, she leaned back and flexed her aching hands.

"What have you got to drink in that poorly stocked kitchen of yours besides whiskey?" Becky asked.

Ronnie hesitated to give up the task of washing Miguel's upper body. It was a task she'd assigned herself while she'd watched Becky do the bandaging, and she found it comforting because she told herself it gave him ease, even in his unconscious state. She could have sworn she'd actually felt the blade bite into her own side, the needle puncture her own skin. His pain had become hers, and now she shared in his relief.

"There's coffee," she said as she dropped the cloth into the bowl of warm water. "And orange juice, of course."

"Coffee for me, and orange juice for you." Becky stood and rubbed the kinks out of her back. "If you're going to nurse this boy back to health, you're going to have to feed him real food, honey. You never have anything in that refrigerator but orange juice and shriveled carrots."

"I'd hardly call him a boy," Ronnie said as she admired the broad back of the man who now rested peacefully in her bed.

"They're all boys when they're sick. And this one's going to be laid up for a while." Becky frowned. "Do you think his enemies would have any way of tracing him back here?"

"I don't see how." Ronnie came around the bed and linked her arm with Becky's. "I'll make you some coffee if you'll help me solve my next problem."

"Which is?"

Ronnie stepped aside and let Becky precede her down the steps. "I've got to make a quick run to De Colores, which means—"

"Which means you want me to watch over this fellow. Now listen here, missy, this old girl retired from dressing wounds and carrying bedpans a long time ago."

"Bedpans?" Ronnie wondered how she would improvise an article like that.

"You don't like the sound of that too much, do you?" Becky grumbled as she approached the descent slowly and at an angle, in deference to her creaking joints. "Every time you brought home a stray puppy or a lost kitten and your dad got after you for it, you always brought it to my house. And then who ended up taking care of the darn thing?"

It had never occurred to Ronnie that Becky might turn her down. The old woman never had. Ronnie explained the problem of her soon-to-be-stranded passengers over sandwiches and coffee. Since McQuade and Elizabeth had planned to take a fishing boat from Arco Iris to De Colores and they hadn't yet hired one when she'd last seen them, she figured she had another day or two. But she'd promised to be there for them when they needed her, and she couldn't risk cutting it too close. She wanted to leave the following afternoon. Becky agreed to stay with Miguel while Ronnie was gone, but she was bent on retiring again, at least for the night.

After Becky left, Ronnie climbed the stairs to her room. The house that had once housed four people now had only one bedroom. It had never been big enough for four, but after her brothers had left home and her father had moved to Marathon Key, she had turned the bedroom downstairs into an office, and remodeled the attic, adding a small bathroom up there. The tiny room that had once been hers was now used for storage. She was comfortable now, but her redecoration hadn't provided for guests.

Miguel hadn't moved. Ronnie took the small upholstered rocker from its place by the far window and put it beside the bed. She'd had less comfortable sleeping arrangements. This wouldn't be so bad. As tired as she was, she figured she could probably sleep standing up.

A hot shower melted the tension from her shoulders. She wrapped her hair in a towel and dressed in a comfortable pair of pink jersey pajamas. Then she slathered her face with the same camphor-scented cream she'd been using since she was thirteen. The thought of the pretty things Miguel had said about her made her wonder whether it was time for a new scent. She'd doubled her age since she'd first adopted this one. She remembered Elizabeth Donnelly's faint aura of tropical flowers, and the way McQuade's eyes had glittered whenever Elizabeth entered a room. Would Elizabeth have piqued the same interest if she'd smelled like camphor?

Ronnie reminded herself that she was not the flowery type. There wasn't a flower in her wardrobe. She liked to see them blooming by the doorstep, but she wasn't inclined to wear them. That wouldn't be Ronnie. Anyway, what difference did it make? She sat in the rocker and kneaded the coiled towel to blot the water from her hair. She wanted to help this man who had hijacked her plane. That was her choice to make, and it had nothing to do with whether he liked her scent or the color of her eyes.

She liked the color of his, she remembered. But now that they were closed she liked the way his black hair teased his forehead in sexy disarray and the way his long, dark lashes hid the telling circles under his eyes. He looked younger now, free of pain. It was hard to imagine him as a leader in a military coup. Belief that such a man had suddenly ended up in her bed came harder still. Men didn't end up in her bed, nor, for that matter, did she end up in theirs.

Ronnie dropped the towel on the floor, dimmed the lamp, propped her feet upon the bed and rocked gently. The rocker's rhythmic creaking would soon lull her to sleep. The thought flitted across her mind that she had no business sleeping when she had given her word to two people who trusted her. At this moment she was supposed to be somewhere else. But her energy was gone, her mind was drifting and she had no other choice right now. Her body demanded sleep.

Hours later she was awakened by a tortured groan. Miguel had rolled onto his back, and was fighting with the sheet, which was wrapped around his hips like a sarong. Ronnie sat next to him on the bed and called his name, but there was no response. She took his face in her hands and found that his skin was warm and dry. The cool breeze from the open window touched her still damp hair, and sent a shiver through her shoulders.

She fetched a washcloth and a bowl of tepid water from the bathroom. The faint smell of whiskey plagued her as she pressed the cool cloth against his face. Already she regretted the hangover that would add to his discomfort when he awoke, and she couldn't believe the alcohol had spared him any pain. He groaned again as he turned his face away from her.

"*Sediento,*" he muttered.

He was thirsty. She slid her arm beneath his head and reached for the glass of water she'd left on the nightstand. "Drink this, Miguel."

He swallowed several times before he turned his head away again. *"Gracias."*

She laid his head down and wondered whether she should try to give him something for fever. Not yet, she decided. Aspirin was all she had, and it probably wouldn't be good for someone who'd been bleeding the way he had. His eyes were closed, and the water had left his lips looking moist and sensuous. Ronnie imagined herself comforting him with a tender kiss.

The image was absurd, and she shook her head to dispel it. The man was in need of practical nursing, a job she'd never thought she would be much good at. Tomorrow she would turn him over to Becky, and then he would have the best. Ronnie had done what she could for him. She had flown him to a safe place.

He tried to shift his position again, but the sheet effectively restrained him. Ronnie wondered whether it hurt him to lie directly on the wound. She tucked two small pillows under his right side, above and below his bandages.

"Caliente," he whispered between quick, shallow breaths.

Ronnie reached for the washcloth and gave it a squeeze. "I know you're hot," she told him as she began bathing his chest. "You're fevered, and I'm not sure what to do about it. When Becky comes back..." The thought disturbed her. Becky would come back and take care of him while Ronnie replaced the oil she'd drained from the plane's engine. Each woman would perform the task she knew best. Ronnie would feel the oil between her fingers, but she would remember the feel of Miguel's warm skin.

She didn't like the idea of turning him over to another woman, not even Becky. Her thoughts would be with him as she returned to the place where he'd been hurt. She would see to the safety of those who had paid for her services, but she would worry about Miguel, who had gotten her attention with a loaded gun. It didn't make much sense, but there it was. This man's life was in her hands now, and she *wanted* to help him.

She continued to bathe him until he slept quietly again. Then she returned to the rocker, tipping it back and rocking very slightly as she watched him, taking note of the combination of masculine features that made him so handsome. Even before she slept, she drifted in dreams.

Becky arrived at the crack of dawn to check on her patient. When no one answered the door, she let herself in and climbed the stairs to the bedroom. The scene at the top didn't surprise her. Ronnie was curled up like a cat in the rocking chair, and Miguel slept in a feverish sweat.

The touch of Becky's hand on her shoulder interrupted Ronnie's sleep with a start. "What's wrong?" she asked, pushing herself upright as she tried to shake off overwhelming grogginess. "I thought he was doing better. I just . . . dozed off for a minute."

"He's all right," Becky assured her. The pat on Ronnie's shoulder was intended to settle her back into the chair, but it didn't work. Ronnie was already sitting beside Miguel and testing the heat of his skin with the back of her hand. "There would have been nothing wrong with you lying down next to him and getting some decent rest," Becky pointed out. "You're not going to be in any condition to fly today."

"Yes, I am," Ronnie said absently. "What are we going to do about this fever, Becky? He's been like this for hours."

"I'm going to take care of it while you get some rest," Becky proposed. "Why don't you go on over to my house where it's nice and—"

"He's burning up with it," Ronnie said, ignoring Becky's suggestion. "I was afraid to give him any aspirin, but I don't like this fever at all."

"Neither does he." Becky had long since learned to save her breath when Ronnie wasn't listening. She took the glass from the nightstand, refilled it and handed it to Ronnie. "See if you can get him to drink some water. Dehydration could cause real trouble now."

"Water...poses a problem also." Miguel's quiet statement took Ronnie by surprise. His eyes were still closed. His face was damp, but his lips were dry. "There's a bathroom close by, isn't there?"

"In your condition, it'll have to be brought to you," Becky said offhandedly as she turned her attention to the boxes of Red Cross supplies. "We'll give him an aspirin substitute."

"I'll find it," Miguel muttered, pushing himself up gingerly. He wasn't talking about the medicine. By the time Ronnie moved to the opposite side of the bed, he was sitting on the edge, clutching the sheet at his waist.

"What are you trying to do?" Ronnie demanded. "You can't—"

"Trying to spare us all—" he closed his eyes and waited for the room to stop spinning "—further embarrassment."

Becky's chuckle rose from the floor in the corner of the room. "I've seen it all, honey. The last time I remember being embarrassed by any of it was in 1938."

"Spare myself, then." When the dizziness did not subside, he opened his eyes and saw the young woman with the beautiful aquamarine eyes. She stood over him, and the way she squared her shoulders and ducked her head beneath the roof's steep pitch gave him the feeling that she sought to steady the undulating surroundings, much like a tent pole on a windy day. "I can make it," he told her.

"I'll help you," she said, and she lent him her strength once again. He tried to keep himself covered, but the effort was wasted, and the sheet was left trailing over the end of the bed as he leaned heavily on Ronnie for support. She transferred his weight to the sink on one side and a towel bar on the other. She kept her eyes on his face. "You think you can manage, um...by yourself?"

"When we hear a big thud in there, we'll know he managed to pass out," Becky predicted.

Miguel's chest heaved with the effort of his breathing, and his face, drained of color, glistened with sweat. "I need a moment's . . . privacy," he said, laboring over the words. "If you'll just give me that, you'll hear nothing."

Ronnie nodded and closed the door. The man had suffered enough humiliation, and Ronnie knew how the need to salvage what was left of one's pride could create strength where it seemed there could be none left.

"I'll go down and see what I've got in the house to feed him," she told Becky. "What do you think? Soup? Or juice. He drank some juice yesterday."

Becky examined the label of a plastic bottle as she rose from the floor over the protest of morning-stiff joints. "See what you've got. His stomach might not tolerate anything yet, but—" She raised an eyebrow toward the bathroom door. "We'll have to start getting something in him pretty soon."

Ronnie went to the kitchen and rummaged through her cupboards. She found a can of beef consommé that had probably been sitting up there for a year. Leaning across the sink, she drew the blue gingham café curtain back and took time for a good look at the morning. Still rouged by the risen sun, the sky promised her smooth flying. That was good. She wanted to do her job and get back just as soon as she could. She was needed here, too.

She found a pair of clean shorts and dressed quickly in the downstairs bathroom before padding up the stairs on bare feet. Miguel was in bed, braced on his elbow, the glass somewhat unsteady in his hand as he washed down the tablets that had come from Becky's plastic bottle.

"Do you think you could eat something?" Ronnie asked. Easing himself back on the pillows, he offered her the glass. Her cool, steady fingers met the vibrating heat of his, and he hesitated in releasing the item that brought about the contact. His eyes were glazed, and his face looked like a clay casting of itself in an unnatural tone.

"Not now." He tried to smile as she set the glass aside. "It seems I haven't the stomach for this surgery... in the field, as it were."

"Maybe you just can't stomach my dad's brand of whiskey."

"He needs rest," Becky said. "I've given him something to bring his temperature down."

"I did tell you I'd be leaving today," Ronnie reminded him. She knew her urge to apologize for leaving him was silly. She had a commitment, and he had interfered with it. Still, the apologetic tone was there. "I really must get back to the people who hired me. They could be in serious trouble, just like you. I'll be back as soon as I can." Her face brightened with another idea. "Maybe I can get the scoop on who knows what about your untimely—"

"No!" He gripped her wrist with more strength than she'd thought he had. "I can't stop you from going back there, but you are not to express an interest in my fate to anyone. Do you understand? You will not hint of any association with me."

"I can't see how they could possibly find you here, Miguel. You'll be perfectly safe—"

"But you won't be."

Ronnie wondered whether his grimace reflected physical pain or something else. "I've been down there lots of times," she assured him. "I know people there. I'll be okay."

"How do you know?" He gripped her tighter, and the dark heat in his eyes betrayed his anxiety. "We know nothing for certain. You heard a radio report of my assassination. I was told that I had been tried and was to be executed. I may have been seen, and I'm not certain who my enemies are. Someone may have reported your plane." He paused, allowing time for the gravity of the situation to sink in. "What you're doing is foolish."

"Those people are counting on me."

"Send someone else."

She laughed at the very idea. "I'm nobody's boss, Miguel. There's no one to send."

"There must be other planes for hire. Other people who do what you do who wouldn't be—" he closed his eyes and gave a weary sigh "—putting themselves in such danger."

"I was hired for this job, and I'll get it done." He released her, and she stood up. "I have to undo my simulated oil leak and service my engines, but I'll try some of my cooking out on you before I take off today. I'm sure you'll be impressed."

"I'm sure I will." The resignation in his tone was clearly born of complete exhaustion, and he was drifting. "I've been quite impressed so far."

This was not the time for engine trouble. Ronnie had replaced the oil and restored everything she had tampered with for the customs agent's benefit, but the engine refused to crank. She checked lever adjustments, circuits, connections—everything was intact. Left with the sinking feeling that her airplane was in need of major repair, she headed for the phone. Norm Keller, her favorite mechanic at the Marathon aircraft maintenance shop, agreed with her suspicion that she needed to have the starter repaired or replace it with a new one. She knew she couldn't repair it at home, but it wouldn't take much to install a new one herself. Naturally there was not one available at the shop. Norm promised to track one down for her and get back to her as soon as he could. She clapped the receiver down in frustration and turned to find Becky standing in the kitchen doorway.

"Sounds like you might be stuck here a while," Becky observed. "How about some lunch?"

"Is he asleep?" Miguel had become such a constant presence in her mind that she didn't even think to name him.

"He is." Becky smiled knowingly as she passed Ronnie on her way to the refrigerator. "I don't know much about his politics, but I'd say you've rescued yourself a real looker there, missy. Soon as he gets his color back..."

"Oh, Becky!" Ronnie used the toe of one gym shoe to push off the heel of the other one. "I don't care about his looks or his politics. The man was shot in the back. I couldn't just...open the door in midflight and push him out." She remembered considering it, and smiled as she pulled off the other shoe.

"He's right about your going back there, you know. It's too risky."

"I've been paid to take the risk." Ronnie set her shoes and socks near the back door and moved to the sink to wash her hands. "De Colores is just a risky place to be right now, that's all. That's why I probably couldn't get anyone else to do it for me even if I wanted to." She reached for a nailbrush and looked over her shoulder at the woman who knew her better than anyone else. "The woman who hired me had her child taken away from her before she was deported. She's taking an awful chance going back there."

Suppressing the urge to repeat herself, Becky opened the can of consommé and poured it into a sauce pan. If Ronnie couldn't get the plane started, maybe the problem would solve itself, at least on this end. As for Ronnie's passengers in De Colores, well, Becky didn't know them. She hadn't mothered them into adulthood. Ronnie was convinced that their lives depended entirely on her, but Becky had lived long enough to know that no human being truly carried such a burden. Of course, Ronnie hadn't experienced that revelation yet, and she would keep trying.

"It'll all work out." It was, Becky knew, one of those truisms the young were bound to misconstrue or just ignore.

"Of course it will. I'll fix the starter, and we'll be back in business." Ronnie flipped the hand towel over the cabinet door beneath the sink and turned to give Becky a peck on a cheek worn by the years to powder softness. "I don't know what I would have done with him if you hadn't been here, Becky. You're amazing, you know that?"

"He's not out of the woods yet. And I might as well tell you, missy, if he takes a turn for the worse, I'm calling for help."

"He's not worse, is he?" Ronnie's eyes widened as she started backing toward the door to the living room. "Didn't that stuff help his fever any? Has he lost any more blood? Is he vomiting? What?"

"I'm just warning you, now. Actually, he's just been—" Becky shook her head as Ronnie took the steps two at a time the way she had when she was twelve "—sleeping."

Ronnie sat on the side of the bed with her bare feet tucked under her. Even with the cross ventilation from both windows, the garret room was warm. Miguel's muscled torso glistened. She laid her palm against his cheek, and his eyelashes lifted slowly. "My angel is back," he said in a voice that sounded rusty.

"Got my wings clipped," she told him as she drew her hand back. "But only temporarily. I just need a new part."

He took a sleepy stab at smiling. "I see no part in need of replacement."

"Yes, well—" She pulled on the legs of her shorts and covered up a few more inches of thigh. "You haven't heard what the Cessna's doing when I turn the key."

"What is it doing?"

"Nothing."

"Ah," he said. "Does that mean you can't fly off to put your neck in Guerrero's little noose?"

"You're the one he's after, buddy, not me. How are you feeling? Does your—" She cast a pointed glance at the bandages that bisected his torso. "Does it hurt much?"

"Not if I don't breathe." He closed his eyes. "I'm very thirsty."

Ronnie brought him a glass of water and helped him prop himself up for a drink. He rested the back of his head against her shoulder, and she felt his hair's dampness through her shirt. "Becky says you've got to try to eat," she told him. "Just some clear soup for starters. How would that be?"

"Hot," he said when he had drained the glass. "I would prefer something cold and tasteless. Like more water."

"Water won't build your strength back up." She settled him back against the pillows and set the glass aside. "If you start slipping away from us, Becky's threatening to call in medical reinforcements, so you'd better follow orders."

"I had just gotten used to the idea of giving them. Have you seen a newspaper today?"

"No." She smiled and dared to tease him. "Want me to check the obituary column and see if you made it yet? You just want to see if they said nice things about you, right?"

"I would prefer to attend the funeral. The eulogy should be interesting. Guerrero deferred to me for Castillo's, and I spoke of loyalty, honor...dreams for the future." He tried to shift his weight for some relief from his pain. "Guerrero will not come to praise me, and he won't have anything to bury."

"Maybe he's already commissioned a monument." Ronnie reached for a pillow that had fallen on the floor and tucked it behind his shoulders. "Or maybe he's hired someone to erase your name from the history books. Either way, surely he'll give you a decent funeral."

"He'll do his peacock act and perhaps cremate me in effigy." He lifted his hand in a gesture that dismissed the whole idea. "History books are Guerrero's last concern. He'll put guns in the children's hands before he'll give them books."

Becky bellowed from below. "Lunch will be served in the loft if someone's willing to help me carry it up there."

Ronnie was too busy urging Miguel to drink his soup to worry about the sandwich Becky had made for her. For Miguel's part, sleep was more tempting than food, and he finally finished the contents of the mug in the hope of being allowed to drift off again. Another dose of the fever-reducing tablets was all that was needed. Ronnie sat with him until he was sleeping quietly.

She busied herself with Miguel's laundry, taking note of his sizes so that she could pick up a change of clothes for him when she had the chance. The afternoon dragged on with no word from Norm Keller. She finally called him, and found that he was having trouble locating a starter for her particular model. He suggested that if she wanted to hedge her bet, she should pull hers out, bring it to the shop and let him try to repair it. In the meantime, if he found a new one, all the better.

Every bolt, every wire, every screw in the Cessna's ignition assembly became the object of Ronnie's verbal assault as she took it apart. By the time the work was done, it was too late to get the faulty part into the shop before morning. She revised her plans accordingly as she headed back to the house. After they had changed Miguel's bedding and all three had eaten again, Ronnie sent Becky home for a good night's rest with the reminder that her next shift would be a long one.

Miguel had lost track of time and touch with reality. Dreams of hot white sand and the glare of the sun off the water washed over damp white sheets beneath him and the sharp pitch of knotty pine above his head. He heard the report of a pistol one moment and the soft voice of a woman the next. Time was measured not by ticking, but by the constant pulsing ache in his side.

She looked different each time he saw her, and the images blended in his mind. She was at once a candy-sweet girl in pink pajamas and a sassy strawberry blonde making light of his trouble in an effort to make him smile. The sound of the shower had awakened him, and he sorted through all the images he had of her, making bets with himself on which one would emerge when the bathroom door opened. He became impatient with the sound of the hair dryer, enchanted with her lilting, snatchy rendition of an old movie theme and anxious when, for a moment, there was no sound at all.

Then she appeared in a cloud of steam, gowned in white batiste, her hair, gleaming with a freshly washed patina, falling softly to her shoulders. Backlit by the bathroom light, the feminine line of her body was defined in silhouette. Too soon she flipped the wall switch, and the definition vanished. He continued to watch her as he wondered whether this aspect would disappear, too. Her blue eyes brightened with surprise.

"I woke you up." She opened the closet door and took a white duster from a hook. "I'm sorry I made so much noise."

He was sorry to see her add another layer to the airy cotton gown. "I'm glad you did. I can't seem to stay awake."

"It's the fever," she told him as she came to the bedside. "Soon as we get that licked, you'll start eating better, and then I have a feeling there'll be no holding you down." She sat next to him and touched his face. She hardly needed a thermometer anymore, so sensitive had she become to the slightest variation in his body temperature. "I think it's a little better."

"You smell as good as that shower sounded," he said. "It would be good just to feel clean again."

"I've bathed you . . . some." She tucked her hands into the white cotton folds in her lap. "It helps bring your temperature down."

His eyes were bright black and hot with an intensity beyond feverishness, beyond the heat of the night. He held her gaze for a long time. Without touching him again she felt the dampness that clung to his skin and knew the dryness in the back of his throat. She said nothing, but went to the bathroom for water—a glass of it that was cold and a bowlful that was warm. She brought a washcloth, soap and a towel, and when he had drunk his fill of water, she turned him to his side so she could start with his back.

It was impossible not to admire him physically. Becky had said that all men looked the same to her, but Ronnie knew no other man could look like this one. His skin was tan and smooth, and the muscle beneath it was hard. When he lay on his back he closed his eyes, and she told herself it was just as it had been when she'd done this before. But it wasn't. His faint smile told her that what she was doing gave him pleasure. That was fine, she thought. His comforts were few and not to be minimized. She spent much time soothing his face and his chest with water.

A bottle of hand lotion caught her eye. Setting the water aside, she squeezed a dollop of lotion into her palm and rubbed her hands together, releasing the aloe scent. She began kneading the muscles in his shoulders, and his eyes opened sleepily. There was no mistaking the gratitude she saw in them. His skin felt silky as she slid her hands from one group of muscles to another and let her fingertips urge him to relax. He needed real rest. He needed peace of mind. He needed to stop tensing against the pain.

As her thumbs pressed along either side of his spine he groaned and gave in to the relief she offered him. Dream or not, she was a wonder, and such a blessing was not to be questioned or analyzed. The quality of her mercy was unrestrained.

She assumed he'd fallen asleep again, but when she started to move away, he caught her hand. "Tell me your name," he said. "Your true given name."

The soft look in his eyes laid claim to her heart, and her answer came in a whisper. "Veronica."

"Perfect." He closed his eyes again, floating on a dream, the shape of which he managed to verbalize. "Lie beside me, Veronica. I want to be close to you."

Chapter 4

The scant two-foot space on Miguel's left was certainly tempting. Two feet of firm, flat bed. The six-foot length was not quite enough for Miguel, but it was plenty for Ronnie. Her tired body yearned toward the promise of such luxury. He had all the pillows, but she wouldn't need one. Once she achieved a horizontal position, she knew she would be out like a light.

The thought of being that close to him through the night, even when he was in this condition, was somehow very disturbing. His chin, made no less attractive by two days' growth of dark stubble, had dropped to his left shoulder when sleep claimed him. His well-groomed hand, having clutched at the bedding moments ago, now lay relaxed at his side. His legs were too long for the bed, and one foot, extending beyond the mattress, peeked out from the white sheet. But even in this disheveled state, he was clearly a man of distinction. She'd never known a *personage* before—someone whose name cropped up in world news from time to time—but here was one lying in her bed, suffering and sighing, just like any human being who'd been shot in the back. Miguel Hidalgo was a real man. Too real.

For the time being, she had charge of him, but there were moments when she wondered how much charge she had over herself. There were moments when she felt drawn to touch him without any real purpose. There were instances when she caught herself looking at him simply because she enjoyed it. If she let this continue, she was probably in for trouble, she thought. Without really planning to, she gradually lowered her head to the mattress, stretched one leg slowly and eased the other alongside it. Her last conscious thought was of the amount of heat his very real, very human body radiated and how, even from a distance of several inches, she felt it envelop her.

She turned her head, dragging her face across the mattress, and his hand slid from her hair to her cheek. Even half awake, she knew it was Miguel's hand. Her nose was within an inch of his side, and the sheet had slipped to the level of his hipbone. During the night she had managed to scoot halfway down the bed and curl up into her usual fetal position. She moved his hand, carefully setting it on the bed, and raised herself on her arms. He touched her cheeks with the back of his hand, and she felt the warmth of her blush as she looked up at him.

"Good morning, Veronica."

She caught her lower lip between her teeth. Her hair tumbled in her eyes, and she was afraid to imagine how she must look. How *this* must look. She pulled the edge of her duster together between her breasts and sat up quickly, pushing her hair back with her free hand.

"How are you feeling this morning?" she asked.

There was a warm smile in his eyes as he caught the hand coming away from her hair. "Usually when you ask me that you put your hand on my face, like this. How do I feel?"

"Better." She cleared her throat and added, "Not so hot."

He chuckled. "Didn't you just contradict yourself in American terms?"

"Maybe. Better can still be not so hot, and, in your case, not so hot is better." She smiled because, regardless of the wordplay, his face felt good under her hand. "Are you hungry?"

"Yes."

His eyes told her that that exchange was open for interpretation, too. Her thumb stirred involuntarily against his cheek. "You could use a shave."

"That I could."

She jumped up suddenly and whirled away. "Would poached eggs be okay? One of the things I need to do today is get groceries."

"Eggs would be fine." He watched her pull open a drawer and dig through it as though she'd just realized she had an appointment elsewhere. "Did I do something to scare you away?"

"I have to get moving," she answered too quickly. "I have to get to Marathon with that starter and just pray Norm can fix it. We've got to have some food around here, and El—" She cut herself off before divulging the name of the woman who'd hired her. "My passengers are waiting for me. Do you need anything besides a change of clothes?"

"Sunglasses," he said flatly.

"Ah, we're going to convalesce incognito. Anything else?"

"I don't suppose you're a smoker."

"Not a chance." She glanced up. "I suppose you are." He nodded, and she shrugged as she went back to her digging. "I'll get you some cigarettes, then. I would think a man who's just been pointedly reminded of his mortality would swear off—"

"Where did you put my pistol, Veronica?"

She pulled a pair of olive-green shorts from the drawer and looked up slowly. "Why would you need that?"

"Because you are leaving me here with a defenseless old woman, and there are people who want me dead."

"As far as we know, only four people know you're alive," she reminded him.

"As far as we know," he repeated. "Anything we don't know could threaten Becky's life as long as she is with me." He propped himself up on one elbow and looked at her earnestly. "She saved my life. I need the gun to protect hers."

"And your own," Ronnie pointed out quietly.

"Yes. Mine, too."

She opened the closet door. The jacket she'd had with her on the flight from De Colores hung there, and its deep side pocket sagged with the weight of the pistol. She took the weapon out and studied it a moment. She remembered disabling the gun by removing the clip, and then... Where had she put that clip? Her eyes met Miguel's again.

"I think Becky should have the gun," she decided. "If anyone does come after you... well, at least Becky's ambulatory. If I leave her the gun, she won't be defenseless. And she'll defend you." *If I can find that ammunition clip.*

"I don't want her to defend me."

"You weren't anxious for her to carve you up, either, but we were lucky she was here." She laid the pistol on top of her folded clothes and closed the drawer. "Need some help getting to the bathroom?"

After she had Miguel settled back in bed, Ronnie took her clothes downstairs to dress. While she was preparing breakfast, she remembered her lunch bag. It wasn't in the living room, where she remembered dropping it. As she thought it through, she realized that she hadn't hung her jacket up, either. She dug through the trash in the kitchen and pulled out the bag, which yielded the ammunition clip. The eggs were ready. Thinking that she'd tell Becky about it later,

Ronnie dropped the clip into a drawer full of odds and ends, then hurried upstairs with breakfast for her patient.

When Becky came to take her shift, Ronnie took the small boat she shared with Becky and delivered her faulty starter to Norm Keller. She shopped for jeans, shirts, underwear and tennis shoes for Miguel. At a revolving display she tried on several pairs of men's sunglasses, peering at herself in the little mirror and imagining Miguel's Latin features in place of her own. Then she bought groceries, cigarettes and a copy of the *Miami Herald*, and returned to the shop for the bad news that the starter was shot. Norm promised to call her as soon as the part he had ordered for her arrived.

The image of Elizabeth Donnelly's hauntingly beautiful face troubled Ronnie as her little boat bucked the easy rolling water across the channel toward home. Elizabeth must have lost faith in her by now, and McQuade must have been heaping curses on her head. She probably deserved them. Maybe she should have tried to find someone else. But Elizabeth had made it clear that she was not in a position to trust many people, and McQuade, hard-boiled man for hire that he was, trusted no one. What a mess! Ronnie told herself she was crazy for getting mixed up with any of these people as she juggled an armload of packages and shouldered her way through the front door.

"Your father's on his way over."

Two packages fell to the floor as Ronnie unloaded the rest on the small kitchen table and turned a wide-eyed stare in Becky's direction. "Right *now*?"

"He called about an hour ago. Said he stopped in at the shop, and Norm told him UPS had just delivered your part." Becky gave a mock-sweet smile. "He wanted to see you anyway, so he thought he'd run over with the part. You must have just missed him."

Ronnie checked her watch. "I don't suppose it would be a good idea to try to get him over to your house even if we had the time. Not that he'd have any reason to go upstairs, but you never know with Barnaby." Ronnie had followed her brother's lead in calling their father by his first name, and they had all been Barnaby's "buddies." She grabbed a sack of groceries and plunked it on the floor near the refrigerator. Wagging a finger at Becky, she warned, "Don't you dare ask him to stay for supper."

"He'll think it's a little funny if I don't offer."

"I don't care." Hand over hand, Ronnie stashed packages of meat, celery, milk and oranges into the refrigerator in hurried disorder. "Let him think it's funny. He can't just drop in any time he wants and expect people to drop everything. We've got lives, too."

"What we've got is some kind of political fugitive laid up in *your* bed." Becky propped her hip against the counter and stuck her hands in the pockets of her white cardigan sweater. "Maybe you should tell your father about him. I'm not sure we know enough about this man to—"

"No." Ronnie stood up and closed the refrigerator door. "Barnaby would have to report him." She had made her commitment to this man, and she faced

Becky with a look of unwavering conviction. "From the little I know about politics, it seems to me that possession of power is nine-tenths of the law. I can't take the chance that Miguel might be sent back to De Colores, or that Guerrero might send some kind of a hit man after him."

"I think you're taking a very big risk for a man you hardly know."

"I know enough." Ronnie picked up the empty paper bag and folded it up. "How is he?"

"The wound itself looks pretty good. I got him to eat some solid food and gave him what I had for pain. He should be sleeping."

"I guess I'd better warn him about Barnaby." She gathered the packages of clothing and started toward the door. "Oh," she said, doing an about-face when she remembered the cigarettes. "If you see anything else that might start him asking questions, hide it. You know what he's like when he starts playing detective."

Miguel was awake. He watched her ascend the top three steps and cross the room with her armload of packages. Propped up against a pile of pillows, he was wearing his khaki pants and lying on top of the coverlet. It occurred to Ronnie that if she'd had a wounded wolf stranded in her garret, this would be the look in its eyes.

"It's so dark and dismal in here." She dropped her packages in the rocker and reached up to give the cord on the blinds behind the headboard a quick jerk, thereby flushing the shadows away. "Isn't that better?"

He shielded his eyes with his hand and muttered, "I think I may have been a mole in a previous life."

"Is it something serious?" she asked, concerned.

"The doctors say that my eyes are unusually sensitive to light."

"I've got just the thing." Ronnie fished around in one of the bags and produced the black-framed sunglasses she'd finally selected for him. Before handing them to him, she bit off the piece of plastic that held the price tag. He put them on and looked up at her. She tipped her head to one side and smiled. "I knew those were the right ones. They're the kind Fernando Lamas would wear."

"Do I look like Fernando Lamas?"

"A little, especially now that you've shaved." Shaving was something she had imagined herself doing for him, and she wondered if Becky had helped. She pulled out a pair of jeans, followed by a short-sleeved shirt. "But your hair is darker. Actually, you sound like him."

"Perhaps I should forget about that wretched little island and make my way to Hollywood."

"Sounds like a healthy idea if you stay off the freeways out there. Think these will fit?" She set the jeans on the bed and held the shirt up to her own shoulders.

"If you like the voluminous look." He noticed that she had applied a bit of mascara to her blond eyelashes, and, if he wasn't mistaken, she'd enhanced the peachy glow in her cheeks. "The turquoise is very becoming," he said and refrained from adding that it looked much better than the tan shirt she was wearing.

"I wasn't sure about the color." She tossed the shirt across his lap and dropped packages of white T-shirts, briefs and a sweatshirt on top of it. "All I know is that you wear uniforms and don't like them. I couldn't picture you in palm trees and flowers."

He laughed. "Why not?"

"I don't know. It just wouldn't come together in my head." She headed toward the clothes. "Are the sizes okay? I've got tennis shoes and socks in another bag."

He flipped through the pile and checked the jeans. "You did very well. Thank you." He looked at her in earnest. "I will repay you, Veronica. For everything."

The idea made her uncomfortable. She knew that even a friend would expect to be repaid, but she didn't want that. She simply wanted to do this for him. She pulled two packages of cigarettes from the pocket of her shorts and tossed them on the nightstand. "That's the only part of it I want to be reimbursed for. They're not part of the rescue operation."

"I appreciate your thoughtfulness, and I promise to use them only in case of emergency."

"Speaking of emergencies—" Ronnie knelt beside the bed and began folding the clothes and stacking them in a pile "—we don't want to panic, but we may have one coming up. I'm going to put all this stuff under the bed for now. I'm really short on drawer space."

"What kind of emergency?" he asked calmly.

"Barnaby Harper." She stuffed the bags under the bed, too, and then planted her elbows on the bed and tried to muster a reassuring look for Miguel's sake. "My father. He called while I was gone and said he was coming with my engine part. I must have just missed the delivery. And, of course, he just happened to stop in at the shop after I'd left and thought he'd do me a favor."

"It would not be a good idea to tell him about me," Miguel said, and he covered her hand with his. He suspected that it was not easy for her to keep anything from those who were close to her.

"I know." His hand was warmer than hers, but his touch made her shiver strangely inside. She glanced up, and he removed the sunglasses. "My father is the county sheriff."

"I see." He smiled wistfully. "I had better watch my step around you, hadn't I?"

"I don't wear my father's badge." She stood up, drawing her hand away quickly. "Just be very quiet up here, and I'll get rid of him as soon as I can." She started for the stairs and paused. "Try not to listen...I mean, don't pay attention to anything...to the way he sort of treats me like..." She sighed and shook her head as she started down the steps. "Just try to ignore him, okay?"

Barnaby Harper's physique had the look of something formed by a trash compactor. He had a big square chest, short, heavily muscled legs, no waist or neck to speak of, and his white hair was trimmed into the four right-angled corners of a flattop. Totally incongruous with the rest of him, his expressive blue eyes and his finely cut features were the only physical evidence of his relationship to the young woman who greeted him at the door.

"Hello, Barnaby."

"Hiya, kid." Neither offered to kiss the other. "Hear you're having a little trouble getting that puddle jumper started."

She took the box he handed her and set it on the kitchen table. "How do you always manage to be in the right place at just the right time?"

"Intuition." He turned to Becky, who was cracking a tray of ice in the sink. "How's it going, Beck? What have you got there? Iced tea?"

"Would you like some, Barnaby?"

"Love some." He dragged a chair away from the table and sat down. "I don't suppose you're cooking supper, are you, Beck? If you are, I'll consider staying."

"We weren't planning anything special." She glanced at Ronnie as she reached into the cupboard for glasses. "Were we, Ronnie?"

"We sort of had a late lunch," Ronnie told him. "But if you're hungry, I could fix you up a little something."

"That's okay. Your little somethings aren't much better than mine, kiddo." He laughed as his daughter handed him a glass of tea. "Why didn't you ever get Becky to teach you how to cook? Say, are my eyes playing tricks on me, or do I detect a little face paint there?''

She felt her cheeks get warm, and she knew there was no need for any face paint now. ''You've needed to get your eyes checked for years, Barnaby. Last chance, now. You want a sandwich or something?''

He waved the offer away and drank deeply. ''Did you hear about Dan's latest?''

Ronnie shook her head, knowing that her father would tell her about her oldest brother's most recent achievement, probably in his work as a police officer, which Barnaby considered to be the noblest of professions. Her older brother, Rory, was an officer in the Navy, the second noblest profession. Ronnie had always thought she would have ranked somewhere near the top if she had been a Navy pilot.

''He made detective,'' Barnaby retorted. ''What do you think of that?''

''I think it's wonderful.'' She couldn't remember a time when Dan had fallen short of wonderful in her eyes. When she was younger, she'd lived the game of follow the leader, allowing Rory to take the lead whenever Dan wasn't around. She had never pretended to be a boy, but she felt certain there was a female version of her wonderful brothers, and that was who she had tried to be. It had been a futile, frustrating exercise. Finally, with Becky's help, she had given it up and let herself be Ronnie.

''He's gonna clean up in Miami, that son of mine.'' Barnaby planted his elbow on the table with a forceful thud, extending his forearm straight up in the air and positioning his beefy fingers for a hand clasp. He waved at the chair opposite him. "Sit down here and give your old man a go. You can use two hands. Let's see if I can get a takedown in less than a minute."

Ronnie was mortified. What served Barnaby as a normal speaking tone would have carried all the way to Key West. The beautiful man upstairs who had given her eyes such lovely praise was hearing all this!

"I'm not twelve years old anymore, Barnaby," she said quietly. "You win by default."

Grinning, he lowered his arm. "Remember the first time Dan beat me?" He laughed. "'Course, he had the crowd with him. You and Rory really had his adrenaline going." He shook his head, remembering, and then the box caught his eye. "Why were you in such a hurry for this thing? You got a tight booking?"

"I've got passengers waiting in De Colores," she told him as she stood by the counter and stirred her own tea, watching the sugar crystals whirl inside the glass.

"Haven't you heard the weather report today, kiddo? De Colores is in for a bout, and we're gonna have a fair share of wind and rain off the tail end of it."

"You mean . . . a hurricane?"

He closed his hand around the glass, but his attention was on Ronnie as his brow drew down into a scowl. "What's the matter with you, Ron? You're usually the one telling *me* about the weather. I was gonna suggest you and Becky come on back with me.

At the very least, you can count on a power failure out here.''

Ronnie turned to Becky. "You go ahead. I want to put this starter in and maybe move the plane to a safer spot."

Becky returned a meaningful look. "You're overdoing it in the risk department, missy."

Ronnie's eyes glistened like polished turquoise, and her lips were pressed into a firm line. "If it looks bad, I know the way to the shelter. You go on back with Barnaby." She pointed to the blue sky out the window. "I've got time to make my repairs and move my plane," she insisted.

Barnaby opened the refrigerator door and did a deep-knee bend. "Got an orange or something just to... here's one." He tossed the orange in the air and caught it. "Yeah, you've got time. De Colores is out, but you've got time to batten down the hatches here." He reached for a drawer. "Where do you keep the knives?"

Her hand shot out instinctively to block his intended move. "Not that drawer!" They looked at one another for a moment, Barnaby assessing the roundness of Ronnie's eyes. She willed her body to relax as she reached for another drawer. "The knives are in here."

"So what's in there?" He jerked his chin toward the guarded drawer as she handed him a paring knife.

"Junk," she said, "but it's *my* junk. Stuff I save. Stuff you'd probably laugh at."

He did just that without even knowing what it was. He could just imagine. "Such a pack rat. Drawers full of worthless little stuff."

She smiled, mostly with relief. "I never had any room for saving worthless *big* stuff. Except Mama's trunk."

"Yeah." He turned away. The subject of Mama was closed, as always. "Listen, Beck, I'll help you secure your place, and then we'll head for higher ground."

Becky had done all she could for Miguel. The rest was a matter of convalescence, and Ronnie knew how to manage that now. Becky sympathized with Ronnie's other dilemma, but she knew if she left, the decision would be made. Ronnie would not make any foolhardy attempts to race against a hurricane if she were the only one left to take care of Miguel. Her concern for Becky's safety had forced Ronnie's hand. Like everyone else, the couple in De Colores would have to wait out the storm, and Ronnie would become the woman in charge of Miguel's recovery.

"I never did like riding in those light planes," Becky said. "You talked yourself into a job, Barnaby. I always have trouble closing those shutters."

After Barnaby and Becky left, Ronnie took the ammunition clip from the junk drawer, dropped it into her pocket and bounded barefoot up the steps to her bedroom. When she saw the pistol lying on the bed under Miguel's hand, she laughed, releasing an hour's worth of tension, and held the clip up for him to see.

"I know," he said, contemptuously eyeing the useless gun in his hand. "This was all I had. I felt like Jim

Bowie lying in his bed and listening to Santa Ana storm the Alamo.''

"You couldn't have bluffed Barnaby Harper as easily as you did his daughter," she said as she dropped the clip into her pocket again and sat beside him on the bed. He moved over to give her room.

"It was loaded when I pointed it at you," he reminded her solemnly. He knew he would always cringe inside whenever he thought of the time he'd held her at gunpoint.

"You wouldn't have used it, but, of course, I didn't know that then."

"You don't know that now."

"Yes, I do." She hadn't asked him about his temperature, but he was her patient, which meant that she could touch him without asking and without fear that her action would be misinterpreted. She touched him only to help him. He accepted it because he knew that. No big deal.

His face was as warm as the look in his eyes. "There's a storm coming," she said. Her voice had gone husky.

"I know." Her hand felt cool against his cheek, and he wanted her to keep it there. Earlier in the day when he'd gone into the bathroom to shave and wash up, he'd fought off wave after wave of dizziness with thoughts of her hands on him, cooling him, soothing him, driving the pain away. She had a healing touch. He wondered if she knew that.

"How long has it been since you took something for the fever?"

He caught her hand before it slid away. "Check my chart."

"You know, that's not a bad idea." It took real concentration to think of anything but the effect his handclasp was having on her pulse rate. "We should have a chart, or at least a list—"

"I think you'll find one in the drawer there." He nodded toward the nightstand. "Becky's been making notes of some kind. I assume they're of a professional nature."

"She thinks of everything. I should probably try to get her to stay, at least until you're—"

"I'm sure I'll get along quite well under your care." He turned her palm up and filled it with hard, cold metal. "You said you were going to leave this with Becky."

"I know. I forgot about it."

"It's useless anyway without the clip. If you're to be the keeper of the gun, then load it and keep it in a handy place." He smiled as he folded her fingers around the weapon's grips. "You see? Something inside you is still not quite sure of me."

"It isn't that," she insisted.

"It *is* that. It is that I threatened you, and now I must work harder to earn your trust." His hand stirred over hers. "I intend to do that, Veronica. You've more than earned mine."

She rose from the bed, took the clip from her pocket and fitted it into the butt of the pistol, which was set on safety. "I can't hit the broad side of a barn with one of these," she told him as she slid the pistol into the drawer of the nightstand. A piece of paper caught her eye. "My brother Dan tried to teach me once, but I never got the hang of it." Her eyes were fixed on Becky's notes as she added, "Just don't shoot my father. I don't have room for another patient."

"Veronica." She looked up. "You must understand that I can't allow anyone to detain me here. If you leave the gun there, I'll use it to defend myself if I have to."

"My father's going back to Marathon." She considered the intense look in his eyes. "My father's not the one you're worried about, though, is he?"

"No. He isn't looking for me."

"Probably no one is."

"Even if he were, he wouldn't harm you. I think..." He touched her knee and saw the flash of surprise the touch of his hand brought to her eyes. He moved his fingertips back and forth to soothe, to persuade. "I think you should go with Becky and your father. I know I can't go anywhere for a couple of days, and I'm afraid it's not safe for you here... with me."

"I thought you intended to earn my trust."

"I do. You, the two boys who put me on your plane, and Becky. Beyond that, I don't know who my friends are. And I don't want my friends caught between me and my enemies."

A knock at the back door was followed by Becky's call. "We're leaving now, Ronnie."

"If you're gonna get that starter put in, you'd better get moving, kiddo! That front's moving in."

Ronnie flew to the steps, casting a quick glance over her shoulder as she started down.

"Go with them," Miguel urged, merely mouthing the words.

Within ten minutes she was back, carrying a newspaper and two glasses of orange juice. "They're gone. I've got some work to do, so I thought I'd bring you something to read." She set the juice down and handed him the paper with a smile. "Do you like seeing your name in print?"

"Is it extolled or maligned?" he asked as he unfolded the paper.

"I would say that it's extolled for the moment, but soon to be disgraced. Fortify yourself with this." She handed him a glass of juice, and he took it without looking up from the front page. "You'll need it. You're definitely past tense. Assassinated by a rebel faction."

"Three boys," he corrected as he scanned the news. "What did he do to them?"

"Supposedly they're in custody. There's some suggestion that you may have been involved with them, and they turned on you. The investigation continues." Ronnie took her seat on the edge of the bed and sipped her juice.

"He killed them," Miguel said tightly. The pages rustled as he searched for more information. "He'd have to."

"But *they* shot *you*."

"They did what he told them to do." He tossed the paper aside and stared at the window at the opposite end of the garret. "At least, they tried to."

"Miguel," she said quietly, "we're not talking about going on maneuvers. Those men attempted to murder you. How could they possibly have thought a legitimate execution would be carried out—"

"We are talking about three boys who know nothing of due process." He watched the gathering of gray clouds and avoided her eyes. "They know how to cut cane or gut fish or take handouts from tourists, and they know how to do as they're told."

"What about the two boys who helped you?"

He smiled, remembering their faces. Raphael and Paulo. "They were not ordered to kill me."

"They seemed quite devoted to you. I don't think they would have—"

"There's no point in speculating, is there?" He turned to her and realized that her face was as dear to him as any in his memory. "Make me strong, little angel. Strong enough to go back to them."

The rich sound of his voice shimmied through her. "Drink your juice," she told him. "That's my best prescription."

"You're going to fix your plane now?"

She nodded. "Try to get it done before the weather gets bad."

"You're not still thinking of going to De Colores," he warned. "Not now."

"No, not till the storm passes. I checked with the weather bureau, and Barnaby was right. De Colores is getting socked, and without much warning."

"The losses will be great. Homes will topple like houses made of cards." He drank his juice and set the glass on the nightstand. "It's safer for you here, Veronica. Even after the storm is over, you can't go back there."

"There's no point in speculating now, is there?" she said, echoing his remark. She went to the bathroom and brought him a glass of water and a dose of Becky's prescription. "Try to rest while I get my repairs done and move the Cessna to a more sheltered place. Then, if you're really brave, you can take your chances with my cooking."

"I look forward to it. So far it's been excellent."

"Canned soup and orange juice?"

He closed his eyes and smiled. "Excellent."

The sky was dark and heavy when Ronnie returned to the house. She looked like a diesel mechanic. She couldn't even go upstairs without showering in the bathroom downstairs first. Once that was done, she realized that all her clean clothes were upstairs. All except . . .

Wrapped in a thick white towel, Ronnie went to the storage room off the kitchen, where she kept her mother's trunk. She knelt slowly and opened the lid. The scent of the cedar lining caused her to draw a deep breath while she settled back on her heels. Sometimes she opened the trunk just for that smell. She had no real memories of her mother, but she had the trunk. She remembered the day Barnaby had decided to get rid of it, and she had tearfully pleaded with him to let her keep it. The tears seemed to take him off guard since, coming from Ronnie, they were quite rare, and he relented after securing her promise to keep it out of his sight.

The trunk contained pictures, jewelry that was valuable only because it had belonged to her mother, and dresses, including a white wedding gown that attested to the fact that Ronnie shared her mother's size. And there were keepsakes. Trinkets and programs, seashells and satin sachets. Things that were never really needed but were worth saving.

Ronnie unfolded her favorite dress from her vintage collection. The soft shades of tropical jade and turquoise seemed too pretty to wear, but she loved the way the yards of voile fluttered when she shook it out. She'd tried it on many times in private, and it made her feel...different. If she wore it for Miguel—not that she would, but if she did—would he tease her? She remembered Barnaby catching her in it when she was sixteen and dying for a certain someone to ask her to the high-school prom. Barnaby's comment had made her feel like a fool, and the certain someone had asked another girl. A girl who didn't look like "a goose trying to be a swan."

Ronnie pushed her damp hair from her face as she stood with her back to the door and held the dress to her shoulders. Smiling to herself, she closed the trunk and turned, clutching the dress and the towel to her breast, thinking that it wouldn't hurt just to...

She glanced up, and her entire body froze. Supported by the door frame across the kitchen, Miguel stood watching her.

Chapter 5

"Put it on."

Ronnie whipped the dress behind her back, nearly losing the towel in the move. Wide-eyed, she clutched the terry cloth between her breasts and sputtered as though she'd been caught in some terrible act. "It's just an old thing. I...didn't have anything else handy, and I didn't want to wake you."

"It's pretty. You would look very..." He slumped against the door frame, pressing his hand to his side. She noticed the gun in his other hand.

"Damn you." Ronnie grumbled. The dress fell to the floor behind her as she hurried to help him. "What are you doing up, anyway?"

"I heard someone down here." He straightened and tipped his dark head against the white wood. "When you come into the house, you must tell me you're here."

"Who else would be using my shower?" she demanded, adjusting her towel as discreetly as she could manage right under his nose. Thunder rolled in the distance.

"I didn't hear the shower. I seem to drift in and out." She put her arm around him, and he leaned heavily on her shoulders as he tucked the pistol into the back of his pants. "Perhaps if I ate something substantial, I wouldn't feel so..." He waved his hand in front of his face.

"Dizzy," she finished for him. "You lost a lot of blood, Miguel. You're bound to feel dizzy. You can't be walking around any time you please."

"I didn't hear anything. All of a sudden I knew someone was in the house." He shook his head. "I can't take any more of those pills. They make me too groggy."

Struggling between Ronnie and the railing, Miguel managed the stairs. His breathing was labored, his balance not quite steady. Ronnie imagined the strain was enough to keep him from noticing the warm contact between so much of his skin and such a generous amount of hers.

It wasn't. The fresh smell of soap on her smooth skin and the dash of lemon in her damp hair swirled around in his tipsy brain. He remembered the way they'd fallen in a heap the first time she'd helped him to her bed, and the whole vision tumbled over and over in his head—soft skin, cool, damp hair, a towel

unfurled and the tangy scent of lemon. He felt a tug-
ging at his back and heard the pistol clatter in the
wooden drawer. The spinning stopped when Miguel's
head hit the pillow. No one tumbled, and no one lost
her towel, but the delicious daydream made him smile
and reach to touch the smooth curve of her shoulder
before she could draw away.

She sat next to him with her knees pressed tightly
together and her arms wrapped around herself and her
towel. She felt as though every muscle in her body had
formed a compact ball, but the touch of his hand was
an appeal to relax, to let go. "I'll get dressed and fix
something substantial for us to eat." She stood, and
the motion was slow and stiff. "Could you eat beef?
Like maybe a steak?"

A crack of thunder shook the stiffness out of her
and made her jump. Watching her get hold of herself
made Miguel smile. She managed it quickly, refusing
to indulge herself in a moment of fear. "If you shared
it with me, I think I could," he said.

She backed away, her laughter lacking its usual easy
flow. "Once you taste it, you'll probably make me eat
the biggest share."

"If I do, it will be my loss, I'm sure."

Ronnie emerged from the bathroom wearing her
customary tan shorts and a cotton knit shirt that was
a darker version of her peach skin. The boxy shorts
seemed to be her uniform, and after she disappeared
down the steps, Miguel lit a cigarette and imagined
gauzy turquoise and jade spiraling around her slight
body like the smoke that curled above his head. He

had a strange longing to play Pygmalion, to help her set her femininity free.

She wanted it to be good. *Anybody* ought to be able to broil steaks and bake potatoes, Ronnie told herself. She thought she was doing pretty well until another overhead rumble gave way to a resounding crack, and the lights went out. She hurried to the foot of the stairs.

"Miguel?" she called out.

"I'm still here."

"The electricity went off, but don't worry. I've got plenty of candles."

He laughed. "I appreciate your concern, Veronica, but moles are quite comfortable in the dark."

"Moles?" She remembered his aversion to bright light. "Oh, yes, moles. Well, I just didn't want you to be alarmed." Under her breath, she added, "And sneak up on me with a gun."

"The pistol is right where you left it," he assured her.

She scowled. How could he have heard that?

Back in the kitchen, Ronnie resorted to Plan B—the gas grill. Her father always had good results with the grill, and Becky was a grilling marvel. Ordinarily Ronnie would opt for raw hot dogs rather than take the thing out and try to regulate the heat. It wasn't a fancy model. She wasn't a fancy cook, she reminded herself as she carried the steaks out to the porch, where the hot, black jaws of the grill stood open, ready to destroy her efforts. While the food cooked, Ronnie took candles upstairs, arranged a small cluster on her dresser and a few on the nightstand, then promised to be right back with dinner.

One of the steaks looked like tar paper, but the other was perfect. Uneven heat, she decided as she mounted the steps with a tray containing a hearty meal for one. It wasn't really her fault. But there was no way that Miguel would ever see that other steak.

Ronnie set the wicker bed tray over his lap and settled herself in the rocker. "I guess I was pretty hungry," she said, eyeing his food. The smell of charcoaled beef was tantalizing. "I couldn't stop nibbling all the while I was cooking. I just..." She shrugged, unable to actually make the claim that she had already eaten. "So now it's your turn."

"It is." He smiled appreciatively as he moved the napkin to his lap and took up the knife and fork. "I think you've resurrected my appetite. It looks wonderful." More than the aroma of the food, he savored the anxious gleam in the eyes that were the color of his beloved Caribbean. "Come here and sit beside me, Veronica."

"Oh, but I don't want to...crowd you while you eat." She nodded toward the tray. "Is there anything missing?"

"Yes." The warmth of his smile beckoned her. "You promised to share this with me, and I'm going to make you keep your promise." He patted the place on the bed right next to him. "Come to the table."

She moved, tucking one leg under her bottom as she sat down. "I knew you were basically a cautious man. But, I warn you, I have a pretty strong constitution, so you won't be able to tell anything by trying it out on me—" he filled her mouth with a bite of steak, and it took a moment before she could finish the sentence "—first. Hey, that isn't bad."

"Of course not." He cut himself a piece and popped it into his mouth prepared to relish rather than test. "*Delicioso*, Veronica. I've never tasted better."

"Well, neither have I," she marveled. "Isn't that incredible?"

"Not at all."

"I don't do much cooking," she said, the blush of pleasure in her accomplishment rising in her cheeks. "I used to try to make something for Barnaby and my brothers once in a while, but they always gave me so much flak about how bad it was."

"Who took care of you after your mother died?"

"There was a variety of sitters and housekeepers until we got old enough to fend for ourselves. And then there was Becky." Ronnie accepted another bite of steak as she thought about what an understatement she'd just made. *Thank heaven, there was Becky.* "She let Barnaby know right away she wasn't for hire, and then she became part of our family, sort of like having a mother for a neighbor. Crazy, huh? I used to wish Barnaby would marry her so she could move in."

"Why didn't he?"

She shrugged. "I don't know. I guess because he always had another girlfriend. But that didn't stop me from wishing."

"And it didn't stop her from being a mother to you."

She watched him sample the salad she'd made. The candles near the bed cast his face in bobbing light and shadows, and she imagined sitting across the table from him in the dark, private corner of an elegant restaurant. The reverie was like a black-and-white movie, or perhaps an old photograph. And in the photograph the woman was...

"My mother was very beautiful," she confided. "Barnaby says that none of us kids got our mother's looks, but I know from pictures that my hair is the same color as hers was, and I must be about the same... height." She had almost said build, but she knew that fitting into her mother's clothes didn't give her the feminine shape of the woman she saw in the pictures. She wondered why she was telling him any of this. Was it because she didn't fit into the picture of an intimate candlelit dinner with Miguel Hidalgo?

"Did your mother have eyes that change color like the sea?"

She hadn't realized how closely he'd been watching her. "My mother's eyes were green," she said.

"Plain green?"

"*True* green."

He smiled and repeated, "*Plain* green. Not like yours."

"My mother had beautiful eyes," Ronnie insisted.

"I'm sure she did." He cut off another piece of steak and offered it to her. "I like yours."

She took the meat into her mouth and chewed slowly while he watched. He found her frank look of appraisal to be almost as disturbing as the way her lips moved against one another. She was clearly weighing the probability that he was simply flattering her against the chance that he might be expressing himself as candidly as she was in the habit of doing. It took her forever to say, "Thank you."

He knew the art of flattery. He had perfected it and used it with a certain Old World flair. The women he'd known had expected it and taken it for what it was. It had been part of the ritual, a piece of the armor. It surprised him to realize that the compliment he'd paid her had been genuine. Still more unexpected were the hundred others that formed, less of mind than of heart, as he admired the red-gold candle glow in her hair.

"Were you able to fix your engine?" he asked, shifting the conversation to a less personal topic for both their sakes.

"Yes, but not soon enough," she said with a sigh.

"Better to be grounded here than down there." He raised his brow and lifted one bare shoulder. "Unless, of course, you have an affinity for hurricanes."

"Those people were counting on me," she said stubbornly. "I enjoy a reputation for being totally reliable. I don't want to have that ruined by some dumb storm."

"Or some dumb political fugitive." He filled his mouth with a forkful of potato and his eyes sparkled.

"I can't blame you now for being in a hurry to take off when you were bleeding to death," she allowed. "But I do feel pretty queasy inside when I think about letting those people down."

"It's been a long time since I've met someone who took such fierce pride in being dependable. It's a commendable attribute." He reached for the glass on his tray and took a sip. Orange juice with everything, he thought. Strangely, he was beginning to like it. He also liked the way the candlelight flickered across her face. "Providence has a way of looking out for sparrows and for desperate souls," he told her. "Even the dumb ones."

"*Especially* the dumb ones. What I can't figure out," she added after a moment, "is how someone who's as smart as you are could be so dumb about someone like Guerrero."

"And what makes you think I'm so smart?" he asked.

"The way you talk. Spanish is your native language, but your English is better than mine."

He lifted one shoulder. "I have an American education."

"So do I, but I think yours is a few years up on mine."

"I'm a few years up on you in more ways than one," he said, cocking a finger at her. "But there's nothing wrong with your English."

"How old are you?"

Because she had asked so directly, he laughed and answered in kind. "Thirty-seven."

"Really? I never would have guessed."

"I'm dumb for my age," he quipped with a bright glance out of the corner of his eye.

"Only about Guerrero," she hastened to add. "And who am I to say? He was probably a nice guy until the power went to his head."

"I don't think so," Miguel said as he stared thoughtfully at the pink center of his steak. The ominous sound of rolling thunder reminded him of Guerrero's temper. "I've never heard anyone apply the term 'nice guy' to Rodolfo Guerrero. It was Castillo who started our movement. The old farmer whom everyone loved. I followed him because his dreams matched mine, although—" he looked up at her and smiled "—I was not a man of the soil."

"What were you before you became *Colonel* Hidalgo?"

"I was *Professor* Hidalgo." At the word, laughter bubbled in her throat, and he assumed an expression of mock offense. "You laugh? Only a moment ago you said you detected some signs of intelligence. I'll have you know that I was an associate professor of history at the University of Massachusetts before I took up arms against the old regime in De Colores and became a rebel. Then I became a benevolent dictator's right-hand man, and now I'm a fugitive. All in a day's work, I guess." He laid his fork down and started to lift the tray, but Ronnie stopped him.

"Oh, no, you don't. I've eaten more than you have." She situated herself purposefully, crossing her legs Indian style, and began sawing on the remaining steak. "If you ask me, anyone who's studied history should know better than to get mixed up in this revolutionary stuff."

"Really?" He opened his mouth for the bite of meat she was pushing at him, mostly to get it out of his way. "What would you have done in 1776, Miss Harper?"

"That was different."

"Uh-huh. How was it different?"

She scowled as she pondered the question. "Well, for one thing...there was no Rodolfo Guerrero."

"There was a Benedict Arnold."

"And this was a whole big... This wasn't some tiny little..." Her gesture changed from wide to narrow, and then she frowned, exasperated. "What's a *benevolent* dictator, anyway? You know very well there's no such thing."

"Do you realize how much power your president has in time of war?" he countered. "After a war, whom do you elect to be your next president? Your generals, of course." Piqued by the topic, he fell naturally into the roll of lecturer. "A coup is accomplished by force—military force, although, in our case, it was on a rather small scale. Nevertheless, wartime conditions did exist for a time, and a show of force may have been necessary to restore order. Despite Guerrero's objections, I had written a constitution, and we were ready to form a new government. There would have been elections very—"

"You *wrote* a constitution? You mean you just sat down all by yourself and *wrote*—"

He headed off another mouthful of food by taking the fork from her hand. "What do you think General MacArthur did for Japan after the Second World War? And where do you think the United States got its constitution? It was not a divine gift etched on stone tablets. It was written by men.''

''Men,'' she repeated. ''Not one man.''

''I used it as a model.'' He saw her face brighten, and he smiled. ''I think even Ben Franklin would have approved. Does that give me some measure of credibility in your red, white and blue eyes?''

''It's just so hard to believe that I'm sitting here eating steak with a man who's written the constitution for a whole *country*.'' She took the fork out of his hand and resumed her work on the steak.

''Just a *tiny* little country,'' he reminded her, and she winced when the words came back at her. ''What's hard to believe is that you insist upon hand feeding the man who's written a constitution for a whole country.'' But he did accept another bite.

''A man who was an associate professor of history at the University of Massachusetts,'' she recited happily.

''Turned rebel,'' he added.

''Now hunted fugitive.'' She laughed. ''The whole thing is impossible.''

''It's impossible for me to eat another bite.'' He held his hand up, and the expression on his face pleaded for mercy. ''Truly. My *stomach* may become rebellious.''

Ronnie set the tray aside and reclaimed her seat, planting her elbows on widespread knees and her chin on clasped hands. ''Where's your constitution now?'' she asked.

''It was in the top drawer of my desk.'' Miguel settled back against the pillows and hooked one arm behind his head. "By now it has no doubt been reduced to ashes, along with the rest of my papers."

"But you can always rewrite it," she encouraged.

He smiled, enchanted by the way her eyes glistened with excitement. "I think I remember the gist of it, yes."

"Shall I get you some paper?"

"Now?"

"I want to watch you write it. I want to tell my children about it. Or...my nieces and nephews, anyway." She straightened her back as the excitement grew. "I'll hang a sign outside. 'Miguel Hidalgo slept here.' We'll get the house listed in the guidebooks, and we'll have parchment facsimiles of the De Colores constitution for sale in our gift shop."

"Parchment!" He couldn't help laughing, and he winced when it made his side hurt. "I used a word processor."

"Oh, gosh, don't tell anyone that. It'll ruin everything." It was good to see him really laugh, and she laughed along with him.

"Bring me every pen and pencil you can find. I'll make them all collector's items."

"I'm serious, Miguel." She was smiling, but not to tease him. "The idea of actually writing a constitution for your country..." She shook her head. "That's really something."

"None of it will amount to anything unless I get back to De Colores."

Reality brought an end to the merriment. "What will you do then?" Ronnie asked.

"I'll fight Guerrero," he said, knowing it wouldn't be that simple. "There are those who will join me."

"And if you win?"

"There will be none of this interim military government. Castillo was wrong in letting it drag on, and we paid the inevitable price for such a mistake. If I win, I'll offer the people a written constitution, and we will hold a plebiscite. If the constitution is approved, we will elect a president."

"What if you lose?" she asked quietly.

His smile was almost apologetic. "If I lose, your attempts to save my life will have been in vain."

"Then you can't lose." She smiled, her eyes brightening with the promise of his success. "I didn't go to all this trouble over you for nothing."

Before she took the tray downstairs Ronnie put candles in the bathroom and offered Miguel a sink full of hot water and assistance if he needed it. He would have enjoyed soaking in a tub and then letting her lather every inch of his body, but he knew that wasn't the kind of assistance she had in mind. When she returned, he asked her simply if she would wash his back, which he couldn't reach.

Ronnie closed the lid on the toilet and directed him to sit with his back to her. She snipped off the gauze bandaging and removed the pads that covered his wounds. In the dim light she could see the puckering stitches just below his rib cage. "Does it hurt very much?" she asked as she prepared to clean the area with antiseptic.

"The holes persist in letting me know they're there."

"They're not holes any longer. Pretty soon they'll just be a pair of scars. Battle scars," she named them as she daubed around them with cotton. He flinched. "Stings, huh?"

"Mmm, a little." On the end of a chuckle, he added, "When I became a teacher I thought I would miss out on such things as battle scars."

"If you had stayed on campus, you might have. But think of the fun you'll have showing them off. The, um . . . the ladies in your life will be quite impressed."

He smiled secretly. "Ladies?"

"Or the *lady*," she tossed out as casually as she could manage. "Is there just one?"

"At the moment, there is none."

She, too, smiled secretly as she filled the sink with fresh water, took up the bath sponge and applied it to his broad shoulders and smooth-skinned, tapering back.

Miguel closed his eyes and let the water soothe him even as the touch of her hands and the womanly scent of her filled his head with stirring images. At the moment, he amended mentally, there was actually one. He braced his hands on his thighs, which were spread wide over the seat, and let his head fall forward. There was his angel of mercy who had saved him, sheltered him, seen to his repair and now sought to comfort him. Did he impress her? She washed and rinsed him, and the warm water trickled over his shoulder, down his chest and his belly, and disappeared into his waistband toward the place where, God help him, he was as hard as any lusty youth. One tender angel, and he had no intention of tarnishing her halo.

She set the sponge aside. The muscles in his back were tense—probably, Ronnie thought, the result of being stuck in bed so long. He looked as though he'd made it his practice to be physically active. She was untutored in the skill, but she managed to massage him, clearly to his satisfaction, just by attending to his responses. The starch in his shoulders gradually melted under her hands. Finally he dropped his head back and muttered, "*Bueno*, Veronica. It feels so good."

"You've gotten stiff."

His eyes flew open, and when he saw candlelit innocence in her eyes, he chuckled. "More so than I'd realized."

"You're not ready for anything strenuous, but you do need a little physical activity."

"Whatever you prescribe." She could do anything she wanted to do to him right now with those hands, he thought. Her hands were magic.

"We'll get you up more tomorrow," she promised. "And even while you're in bed, there are things you can do."

"I have no doubt." But he rejected his own most pressing suggestion.

"And, of course, things I can do for you."

"You've already done more than you know," he mumbled as he tilted his head to the right. "But far be it from me to discourage you at this point."

"Are you feeling light-headed again? Let's get you to bed. I can do the rest there."

"The rest?"

She looked down at him and smiled. "The bandaging. You look tired."

"So do you." He held on to the sink and stood up slowly. It was best to put an end to such exquisite pleasure before it became painfully tempting to see it through to its natural conclusion.

"Lean on me," she said. "I'll be careful not to touch—" She looked up at him, and the look he returned made her mouth go dry. She swallowed hard, and added almost reverently, "The place where you were shot."

She bandaged him while he sat on the edge of the bed and smoked a cigarette. Miguel watched the pale smoke disappear out the window into the rain-drenched night, and he thought of the rain and wind that were battering his island home. What would the people do when it was over and their homes were gone? There would be so many needs, and Guerrero would take an interest only in the needs he could exploit. There was no one to stop him now. The rain splashed on the windowsill and began streaming down the wall. He put his cigarette out in the ashtray she'd set on the nightstand.

"I'll have to close that," Ronnie said as she followed the direction of his gaze. She pressed the last piece of tape against his skin and moved within reach of the window. "This damp draft wouldn't be good for you, anyway."

"It feels good, but the floor..."

"It's hardly wet." She turned from closing the window and found him watching her. "Rest now. I'll give you some medication after I get ready for bed."

She emerged from the bathroom in her white batiste gown and robe a few moments later. She took him some pills and a glass of water, and she noticed the pants he'd been wearing had been tossed over a chair. He was covered to the waist with the sheet. Soft light and shadow played across his face as he handed her the glass.

"Good night," she said. She took a candle in its holder from the group of three on the nightstand.

He frowned. "Where are you going?"

"Downstairs. I'm going to sleep on the love seat tonight."

"It's made of wicker," he reminded her.

"I know, but—"

"You need rest as much as I do, Veronica." Holding her gaze with his, he spread his hand over the extra space on the bed. "Sleep here."

"Oh, no, I'll be fine down there. I only stayed close by the last two nights because—"

"You'll be fine up here," he promised. "I will be on my best behavior." He gave her a reassuring smile. "I'm in no condition to behave otherwise."

"It isn't *that*," she said, too quickly. "I'm not worried about... It's just that I'm such a squirrelly sleeper."

"Squirrelly?" The comparison amused him. He could almost see her scampering barefooted up a tree, a silky, pale red ponytail bouncing behind her.

"I move around a lot. I might keep you awake."

He shook his head slowly. "I feel just as tired as you look. Nothing could keep me awake." He moved to give her more room. "Stay beside me, Veronica. It's good to know that you're close by."

She could not deny him that measure of comfort. She blew the candles out, lay next to him on top of the sheet and pulled the bedspread over her.

A sharp crack shattered his sleep. He shouted and sat bolt upright. Pain as jagged and sharp as the lightning that streaked across the sky gouged his side. He clutched himself, groaning, knowing he'd been hit again. Quick light filled the room and was gone before he got his bearings. He shuddered with the sound of cannon fire overhead.

"Miguel," a soft voice called. Puffs of breath warmed his back, and a gentle hand caressed his arm. "Miguel, it's all right. It's the storm."

Stifling another groan, he turned his head toward the voice. She was a dark shadow framed by the window behind her. A flash of lightning formed a curve of white light over the top of her hair. "Veronica?"

"Yes," she whispered as she pressed his shoulder back. "Be careful. You'll hurt yourself."

"I've been...shot." He laid back on the pillow and closed his eyes in his confusion. "My own people... shot me."

"No, Miguel," she said, her soothing voice gradually claiming the operative track in his dream-muddled mind. "Guerrero's people shot you. Are you okay? Did you—"

"It happened again."

"You were dreaming." She stroked his face and found him feverish. "I'll get you some aspirin."

He grabbed her wrist when he felt her moving away. "No, don't go. I'll be on my best . . . behavior."

"I'm not going far," she promised, petting his shoulder even as she disengaged herself. "I'll get you some water. Your throat sounds dry."

He took the aspirin and eagerly drank the whole glass of water, but he wouldn't let her leave the bed a second time. She set the glass on the nightstand and lay beside him again. Another flash of lightning brightened the pattern of knots in the pitched ceiling, and a report of thunder followed.

"It sounds a little like gunfire, doesn't it?" He asked the question hesitantly, dreading that his notion would sound utterly foolish if she disagreed. But he took the risk because he needed her affirmation. A moment ago he'd experienced it all again. The reality had been a nightmare, and the nightmare had seemed absolutely real. He was still shaken, still not certain he could separate the two.

"It does," she said. In the dark, her voice didn't sound as though it belonged to her. It was someone else lying next to this beautiful, haunted man. "It scares me, too."

He was older, stronger, wiser, more experienced—
it was important that she believe in him. He wasn't
sure why, but, at the moment, reasons were immaterial. "Would you mind if I held you?"

"No," she said quietly. "I wouldn't mind."

Chapter 6

The storm wrapped a gray curtain around the house. Without electrical power, the day seemed like a throwback to another time. There was little to distract from the pane-rattling wind, the sheeting rain and the day's heavy darkness except the company of another person. But the two people who shared the sanctuary had slept together the night before. Throughout the day they were aware of little else.

In daylight, gray as it was, it all looked different. They made careful conversation or sat together in uneasy silence. Miguel refused to be bedridden, but his energy was limited. He dressed in his new jeans and a white T-shirt and ventured downstairs to look for reading material. Ronnie behaved like a clerk in a bookstore—a friendly, helpful stranger. And Miguel

was equally polite. He asked permission to open the
window behind the wicker love seat and have a cigarette, and Ronnie quickly assured him that would be
fine.

It was too dark to read the coffee-table book about
the air war in Europe in 1942. Miguel's mind drifted,
like the curling thread of smoke from the cigarette he
held between his fingers, toward something fresh.
Veronica. Lying against his good side, she'd been a
balm for his wounded one. In her sleep, she'd turned
to him, nestling, and he'd felt her heart beating close
to his. He'd thought of opening the cotton robe she'd
worn to bed and letting the tips of his fingers slide
down her throat, her chest, beneath her nightgown in
search of her breast.

It was foolish to tease himself that way. They had
offered one another comfort when the night and the
elements had joined forces to play tricks on the mind.
He knew that, by morning's light, she'd realized that
in the dark of night, she'd come too close for comfort. She was a sensible woman. Giving comfort in the
dark was risky, and Veronica had already taken more
than enough risk in helping a man whose destiny
linked him with a viper.

He watched the smoke slide quickly through the
narrow window and heard a clattering in the kitchen.
She was tempting, and he had to remember that she
didn't mean to be. She had no idea how lovely she was.
When she wasn't feeling wary, as she obviously was
today, she was beautifully natural and naturally caring. Then she was vulnerable. He'd seen the way she

looked at him sometimes, and he knew how many ways a man could use that vulnerability to his own advantage. On the other hand, a man could hold it dear and make every effort to let her see herself in the mirror of his eyes.

"Is the book any good?"

Miguel turned from the window and looked up at her as he reached past the arm of the love seat to put his cigarette out. "It has nothing new to say." He'd actually read very little of the book that lay open in his lap.

"It's one Barnaby left behind," Ronnie explained. "There are others around. Barnaby is a real military buff."

Miguel closed the book and set it on the table. "Do you need any help in the kitchen?"

"Nothing works." She busied herself unloading a pile of magazines from the chair across from him. "Isn't it amazing how many things you forget are electrical? It's a good thing I've got that gas grill."

"There's room for you over here." She hugged the magazines to her chest and lifted her chin, but she made no move in his direction. "I think we need to put an end to this awkwardness," he said. "We have to talk."

Ronnie put the magazines in the chair and took the seat beside him. "How are you feeling? Are you . . ."

He took her hand and pressed it against his face. Her fingers felt cool against his skin even though he was no longer fevered. "I've come to expect you to touch me when you ask that," he said in a smoky tone.

Her fingers moved slightly against his smooth-shaven cheek. He released her hand, and hers lingered a moment before she drew it back. "There was a time when you couldn't answer. Now that you can, there's no need for, um . . ."

"There's a need." She looked straight into his eyes with more curiosity than surprise, and he responded with a hint of a smile. "You're a desirable woman, Veronica. I would be less than honest if I didn't tell you that. Because I don't think you know it."

"I'm a woman, and at the moment—" she lifted one shoulder "—I don't have much competition."

"We could go to any city you care to name. In a crowd of women, I would single you out and offer you a seat next to me."

She gave a toneless whistle. "Wow!" It took a quick shake of her head to clear it of the rich echo of his voice. "I *would* get stuck here without power, without any lights, all alone with some guy who looks like he belongs on the cover of *Gentleman's Quarterly* and talks like Rudolf Valentino."

Miguel tipped his head back and laughed. "Valentino! He didn't even talk."

"That's because his lines were too good to be true, just like yours, professor." She was smiling, more relaxed now, her eyes alight with her teasing.

"Consider the situation from my point of view," he suggested, his smile becoming a counterpoint to his instructional tone. "Like you, I find myself stranded with someone who is both physically attractive and perfectly charming. But I have been literally shot full of holes. A trip to the bathroom is a major achievement. I'm lucky to be able to chew my own food." He wagged his finger at her when she giggled. "Don't laugh at me, woman. You'd do it for me if I asked you to, and you know it."

"I would not!"

"Ah, my sweet angel, you know very well you would. I'm getting stronger, thanks to you, but not strong enough, not yet." The laughter in his eyes disappeared, and it was replaced by soft, bittersweet regret. "And when I am," he said, "when I *am* strong enough, I will leave you unharmed. I promise. We've shared some very intimate moments, you and I, but our circumstances have left us few choices. Please don't be embarrassed, Veronica. Don't be afraid to look at me or talk about what happened last night. We shared a bed."

Her merriment dissipated, and she glanced away. "We can't do that again."

"Why not? It's the only one in the house."

"It's too..." She took a deep breath and expelled it slowly. "Too much. It's just too much."

"Too much what?"

"Too much you. Too much me. Too close together."

"I enjoyed being close to you, Veronica." She gave him a look that invited him to touch her, and there was nothing he wanted to do more. He resisted. "You're much more than a desirable woman." With a shrug he gathered his cigarettes and matches from the side table. "It wounds my ego to admit it, but my lack of physical strength renders me totally harmless."

Her smile was back. "Heaven help us, the man is wounded again. We'd better get you back to bed."

"Oh?" He watched her stand up, then accepted the hand she offered him. "To tend to which of my wounds?"

"All of them." She tugged on his hand. "Your body needs rest, and those dark circles under your eyes can't be good for your ego."

"Nonsense," he said as he hooked his arm over her shoulders. "They're like the battle scars. They garner feminine sympathy."

He woke to the sound of her footsteps on the stairs, and his first thought was that she was wearing shoes. The rain was still washing against the window pane, but it had grown dark, and there were more candles burning on the dresser. He'd slept through the afternoon again and hadn't heard her moving around until now. Ordinarily a light sleeper, he was almost embarrassed by this uncharacteristic behavior. Worse, it left him feeling disoriented, and he was uneasy because so much time had passed while he lay completely unaware of everything that was going on around him.

The sight of her banished all thoughts but one. Veronica. She could have been dressed in sea foam. The dress was like a frothy watercolor, a blend of jade and turquoise that crossed over her breasts, was cinched at the waist and then became a waterfall of

PLAY THE "LUCKY 7" SLOT MACHINE GAME!

NO COST! NO OBLIGATION TO BUY! NO PURCHASE NECESSARY!

PLAY "LUCKY 7" AND GET AS MANY AS SIX FREE GIFTS...

HOW TO PLAY:

1. With a coin, carefully scratch off the silver box at the right. This makes you eligible to receive one or more free books, and possibly other gifts, depending on what is revealed beneath the scratch-off area.

2. You'll receive brand-new Silhouette Intimate Moments® novels. When you return this card, we'll send you the books and gifts you qualify for *absolutely free*!

3. Unless you tell us otherwise, every month we'll send you 4 additional novels to read and enjoy. If you decide to keep them, you'll pay only $2.49* per book—that's 26¢ less per book than the cover price! There is *no* charge for shipping and handling. There are no hidden extras.

4. When you subscribe to Silhouette Books, we'll also send you additional free gifts from time to time, as well as our newsletter.

5. You must be completely satisfied. You may cancel at any time simply by writing "cancel" on your statement or returning a shipment of books to us at our cost.

*Terms and prices subject to change without notice.

You'll love your elegant bracelet watch— this classic LCD Quartz Watch is a perfect expression of your style and good taste— and it is yours FREE as an added thanks for giving our Reader Service a try.

PLAY "LUCKY 7"

Just scratch off the silver box with a coin.
Then check below to see which gifts you get.

YES! I have scratched off the silver box. Please send me all the gifts for which I qualify. I understand I am under no obligation to purchase any books, as explained on the opposite page.

240 CIS YADC

NAME

ADDRESS APT

CITY STATE ZIP

7 7 7 — WORTH FOUR FREE BOOKS. FREE BRACELET WATCH AND MYSTERY BONUS

WORTH FOUR FREE BOOKS AND MYSTERY BONUS

WORTH FOUR FREE BOOKS

WORTH TWO FREE BOOKS

Offer limited to one per household and not valid to current Silhouette Intimate Moments subscribers. All orders subject to approval.
PRINTED IN U.S.A.

DETACH AND MAIL CARD TODAY

DETACH AND MAIL CARD TODAY

BUSINESS REPLY CARD

First Class   Permit No. 717   Buffalo, NY

Postage will be paid by addressee

SILHOUETTE BOOKS®
901 Fuhrmann Blvd.,
P.O. Box 1867
Buffalo, NY 14240-9952

NO POSTAGE
NECESSARY
IF MAILED
IN THE
UNITED STATES

fluttering fabric over her slender hips. Her hair curled softly at her shoulders, and the heels of her sandals clicked against the floor as she brought the dinner tray to the bed. As she came closer, he saw the uncertainty in her eyes.

"Forgive me." Miguel spread his hand over his bare chest as he braced himself on one elbow. "I'm not dressed for dinner."

"You told me to put it on." She set the tray on the bed and stepped back. "Tell me the truth. Do I look silly?"

"Am I laughing?" She saw the appreciation in his eyes and knew that it was not for the food. He hadn't even looked at the tray. It was she who laughed as she shook her head and sat beside him on the bed. He said the words he knew she'd heard too seldom. "You look beautiful."

"I'm sure it's out of style."

"Beautiful can never be out of style."

"It was my mother's. That's how outdated it is." She smiled easily now, her nervousness gone. "I like to put it on sometimes when nobody's looking, just for fun. Do you like chicken cooked on the grill that way?"

"Chicken?" He looked down at the tray and pushed himself up straighter. "Oh, yes, it looks delicious."

"If we had electricity, I could have made lasagna. I'm pretty good with lasagna."

"There's only one plate."

"But lots of food." She smiled as she scooted closer. "I could only fit one plate on the tray."

"And one fork?" He picked up the utensil as if to examine it, then raised a teasing eyebrow as his mouth twitched with the urge to break into a broad grin.

"Gunshot wounds aren't contagious, and I'm trying to keep the dishwashing chores to a minimum."

"I offered to help."

As she watched him puncture the breast of chicken with the fork, Ronnie prayed that nothing red would gush forth. She breathed easily when he sliced into the meat with his knife and it proved to be done. "This was your first day up, and I didn't want any mishaps," she told him. "You were pushing pretty hard as it was."

"I slept all afternoon. Forgive me for taking the first bite, but this is irresistible." He filled his mouth and reported an enthusiastic "Mmm, *excelente*!" as he cut a piece for her. "You can stop apologizing for your cooking, Veronica. You have no electricity to work with, and still you're able to serve a wonderful meal."

Her eyes were soft with gratitude. "Maybe I should just chuck the stove."

"Maybe you should disregard past criticism and take the word of a man who appreciates fine food."

"Okay," she said hesitantly, "but don't expect this every time. Sometimes it just doesn't turn out. Besides, we'll have to rely on canned stuff pretty soon. The frozen food is thawing out, and it won't keep."

"The storm can't last forever." The look they exchanged spoke of mutual regret. The storm had prevented her from leaving him, and they were enclosed by it now, together. No matter what havoc it had wreaked outside the walls of Ronnie's house, it had served their own two-person world quite well.

"You need more time," she said. "I know you're thinking about going back, but you need more time."

"Perhaps another day or two."

"And you'll need help. You can't just storm the presidential palace with two men."

He lifted the glass of ever-present orange juice. "I'll have to find some means of transportation first."

"I'll fly you down there when you're—"

"No, you won't, Veronica. It's too dangerous for you. I know a man in Miami who might be able to help me." He trusted Mikal Romanov, but Mikal lived somewhere in the Midwest. McQuade, who had stood by Mikal during the hostage crisis that Guerrero had engineered a year ago, lived in Miami. Mikal had negotiated the release of the hostages, and McQuade, working with the Red Cross, had been on hand to run interference for him. Miguel thought he could trust McQuade, too.

"We've got plenty of time to talk about it," Ronnie said lightly as she took a turn with the knife and fork. "It'll be a while before you can hook up with anyone from Miami."

"Yes," he agreed, anxious to turn the conversation back to the present. "A while."

They finished their shared meal with no more references to the future. By the time Ronnie set the tray aside, she had kicked off her shoes and become Miguel's vision of a barefooted sea nymph. The lighthearted sound of her laughter drove thunder into the background, and her honey-toned skin glowed in the candlelight.

"No one ever calls me Veronica," she told him. "It always seemed like kind of an elegant name, and I always thought if I ever wanted to be elegant someday, I might use it."

"Do you mind if I use it for you?"

"Oh, no. It sounds so pretty the way you say it," she assured him with a gamine smile. "Say it."

"Veronica."

"Veronica," she repeated with a flourish, and he laughed at her version of his voice. "My mother named me," she said. "Maybe she thought I'd be a movie star or something."

"I thought perhaps you were named for a saint. We De Colorans name our children for saints, and we believe the name influences the child's life." He reached for a cigarette, then thought better of it. He didn't want her to back away from him. "Yours certainly has."

"Has it?" She moved to the side of the headboard and opened the window. The scent of rain-fresh air drifted over them. "Was there a Saint Veronica?"

"Legend has it that when Jesus bore his cross through the streets of Jerusalem, Veronica came forward to wipe the sweat from his face. She was a courageous and compassionate woman." Ronnie took the cigarettes from the nightstand and handed them to him. His warm gaze met hers as he accepted the package. "And you are very much like her."

The strange notion tingled in her system like a message of great import sizzling along telegraph wires. She tried to remind herself that this was just the way Miguel talked, but a stubbornly romantic part of her refused to listen. The compliment was too beautiful to be ignored.

The unlit cigarette was halfway to his mouth when he paused with it. "I don't want this to drive you away," he said.

"It won't. My father always liked to have one cigarette after supper." The quick flare of the match released a familiar sulfur smell that reminded Ronnie of past supper-table scenes. The tip of Miguel's cigarette glowed in the shadows as he drew the smoke deeply into his lungs. Watching made Ronnie's own chest hurt. "I grew up in a house full of men." Even as she said it, she was unsure what that explained.

He turned his head and directed his smoky breath toward the window. "You have one brother who is a very good policeman."

Recollections of her father's recent visit made her blush. "As far as my father is concerned, my mother was the only real woman in our family."

"Then your father is a blind man." Miguel shifted his position just enough to ward off the stiffness that was setting into his side. "Perhaps he chooses to be blind rather than to be reminded of his loss."

"His loss of what?"

"Your mother. You undoubtedly remind him of her. Perhaps he protected himself by thinking of you as one of the boys." He watched her consider the possibility as he brought the cigarette to his lips again. "How many brothers do you have?"

"Just two. And they were right, you know. I was never much good at girlish things."

"What girlish things?"

"Well, like makeup." She smoothed her skirt over her thigh.

"You don't need it."

"It's a good thing." Her eyes sparkled as she laughed, letting him know his words gave her a good feeling. "I used to experiment with it and come out looking like a clown."

His smile was warm. "The dress is beautiful on you, Veronica. It makes me think of dancing."

"Dancing?" She said it as though she didn't recognize the word.

"In the islands, beautiful women and dancing simply run together in a man's fantasies."

"Hey, I can rock and roll like nobody's—"

He shook his head, laughing. "You'll ruin the fantasy. I want to hold you in my arms and move with you to the music."

"I used to practice moving to the music in front of that mirror over there." She nodded toward the full-length mirror attached to her closet door. "When no one was looking, of course."

He blew a stream of smoke past the ashtray as he leaned over to stub out his cigarette. "Wouldn't you rather dance with a man than a mirror?"

"Now?"

"No one is looking."

She glanced over her shoulder as if she weren't sure. "But there's no electricity, no mu—" Her eyes brightened and her hair swished past her shoulder as she turned excitedly back to him. "I've got an idea," she said. "Wait here."

He chuckled as he watched her fly to the stairs on small bare feet. "I'll have to. I can't move that fast."

The quick patter of her feet announced her return moments later. Her skirt fluttered back as she hurried to the bed carrying a silver box in both hands. "Needs no batteries," she quipped as she set the old-fashioned powder box on the nightstand. "It was my mother's. Actually, my *grand*mother's." She lifted the lid and released the tinkling tones of "The Skater's Waltz."

Miguel swung his legs over the side of the bed and stood up slowly, willing the insidious wave of dizziness away. He took Ronnie's hand and raised it to his lips while his dark eyes sent a tender message. "Will you do me the honor of dancing with me, *señorita*?"

He took her in his arms before she could answer, and she felt as though she had stepped out of her body and into a form that defied gravity. She lifted her chin and found her lips to be a hairbreadth from his smooth shoulder. "I'm not wearing any shoes," she whispered, half thinking that might explain why she felt so light.

"Neither am I." He smiled down at her. "We're both safe."

He wasn't wearing much of anything, and she was profoundly aware of that fact. She glanced past his arm and caught a glimpse of the seat of his jeans as

they passed the mirror. It seemed strange that such elegant steps could be taken in jeans. On the next turn,
she saw the dim reflection of a woman with flowing
hair, floating skirt and shining eyes. She actually felt
feminine enough to *be* that woman.

"You must have practiced waltzing in front of the
mirror," Miguel said close to her ear. "You do it very
well."

"I'm waltzing?" Her body was doing whatever his
suggested and feeling decidedly ardent about it.

"We're waltzing. I hope you'll pardon my attire,
but I thought that since dinner was informal . . ."

"Denim and gauze are in this year," she assured
him. "Especially for the gentleman who's convalescing."

"*Most* especially if he's convalescing in the lady's
boudoir."

Ronnie relished the sound of his deep chuckle, and
she closed her eyes and found herself smiling against
his shoulder as she pivoted, her bare foot brushing
against his.

"*Perdone,*" he offered gallantly. "Excuse my
clumsiness, *señorita*. One would think I'd been shot
in the foot." He turned his lips to her hair and savored its lemon scent.

She caught her breath for a moment, then managed a lighthearted comeback. "Such flawless man-
ners, *señor*. You'll soon have me thinking I could
replace Ginger Rogers."

"I've never danced with Ginger Rogers," he said in
a voice that sounded throaty so close to her ear. The

notes from the music box were winding down, and they moved with them in slow, hazy motion. "Does her hair smell like lemon?" he whispered.

"It probably smells like something more—"

"You replace no one, Veronica." With the final tinkling note he placed her hand on his shoulder and lifted her chin in the curve of his finger. "Your own place would be empty if you did."

The candlelight shone in her eyes, and he thought of moonbeams in a calm sea as he lowered his head. A brief kiss, he thought, just to show her, tell her... taste her, ah, feel her lips...such soft, eager lips. Like an unexpected shock, the kiss caused a quick spark, and each looked to the other. *Did you feel that?* Her eyes said yes, and he dipped his head with no equivocating notion in his brain. There was only the need for another kiss. Hard, wet, open, demanding. A jagged shaft of white heat shot through them, and then the resounding report seemed to echo in the night.

Ronnie gripped the warm, solid ledges of his shoulders as she rose on tiptoe to meet his kiss. His arms tightened around her, and he moved his feet apart to allow her to step between them, bringing them closer still. He moved his hands over her back, now caressing her through the thin fabric of her dress, now dipping into the deep vee to touch the long, sleek indentation of her spine. He kissed her until she was dizzy with it.

So was he. He raised his head and drew a deep, unsteady breath. *"Gracias, señorita.* You're a wonderful dancer."

"I'm beginning to believe you." She opened her eyes and smiled. "It's almost like flying."

"I think I must make my landing soon."

"Oh, Miguel," she sympathized, suddenly coming to her senses as she ushered him back to bed. "You keep trying to overdo it, and I'm obviously not helping matters. Becky said that what you had was just like major surgery, and here we are—"

"Dancing." He eased himself against the pillows and drew her by the hand to sit beside him. "Another ego-wounding experience. One turn around the dance floor and I'm—"

"Kissing." She made him look at her, made him listen. "We were kissing, Miguel. That's a step beyond dancing."

"Yes, it is." He pressed his lips against her fingers. "Another kiss. You warm my heart, Veronica, and I want to kiss you. But my word is good, you know. I won't hurt you."

She glanced away. "A gentleman of the old school."

He ignored the remark. He had been raised a gentleman, but he had never felt the concerns he felt for this woman. He wanted to don armor. "Nor would I allow harm to come to you if it were in my power to prevent it." He chided himself immediately, but, by God, that was the way he felt.

"Pretty big talk for a man whose color just drained from his face after a couple of minutes of dancing."

This was the time to assume a casual posture, she thought. The man had moved from a kiss's heady promise to talk of not hurting her within the space of a few breaths, and she wondered if she'd missed something along the way. Was she supposed to feel threatened? Perhaps it should embarrass her that she didn't.

"Kissing," he reminded her. "Much energy is expended in kissing a beautiful woman."

"More than you could spare, obviously." He was still holding her hand as though the contact came naturally to them. The butterflies in her stomach reminded her that it didn't.

"Get ready for bed." He smiled as he moved his thumb across her knuckles. "And you must put this dress in your closet, Veronica. Don't bury it in a trunk."

Her ears were still stuck on *Get ready for bed*. Beyond that, she heard only the wind as it whistled under the eaves. Without even giving it voice she rejected the idea of sleeping downstairs. She wanted to be with Miguel. She wanted him to hold her through this stormy night, and she wanted to rest in the knowledge that he was all right. His health had become her responsibility, her focus. She would stay close and watch over him.

She dressed in her pink pajamas and returned to the bed after blowing all the candles out. Miguel had fallen asleep. A spring groaned beneath Ronnie's cautiously planted knee. She took such care in easing herself down beside him that the kiss he nuzzled at her temple took her by surprise.

"Sleep well, *mi angel*."

She tried to wake him as carefully as possible, but he heard the urgency in her voice even before the words, "Miguel, wake up," made sense to him.

He sat up quickly, and the pistol materialized in his hand. He groped for his bearings and demanded, "What is it?"

"Not—no, it isn't that, Miguel." Ronnie laid a reassuring hand on his forearm. "I'm sorry. I didn't mean to alarm you. It's just that it's stopped raining, and I want you to see the sky."

"The sky?" He leaned back on his elbows with a belated awareness of the stiffness in his side. Blood pounded up the side of his neck, and his temples throbbed. He lowered the gun. *Dios. The sky?*

He noticed, as Ronnie rushed to the closet and pulled out a shirt, that she was already dressed. "Put this on," she insisted, tossing him the shirt whose color reminded him of her eyes. "Hurry, or it'll be gone."

"The sky will be gone?" He struggled with a combination of stiffnesses—his body's and that of the new cotton shirt.

"No, the . . . you have to see it," she insisted as she helped him with the shirt.

"Where did you put my shoes?"

"No time for shoes." She dragged him to his feet. "On second thought," she said as she snatched the tennis shoes from the dresser on their way by, "you might catch a chill."

She forced herself to contain her enthusiasm and slowed her steps to match his pace. She maneuvered him out the back door and across the sandy yard, where tufts of thick-bladed grass were the only growth hardy enough to survive. Sea oats, already on the rebound from the pounding rain, sprouted along the path to the beach. Not a tree meddled with the expansive melding of sea and sky. A single pelican stood in silhouette atop a purple dune, and beyond him the sky was lightening in rosy hues. Harmless lavender clouds billowed above the deep magenta crack above the horizon, which spilled a river of pink into the calm blue-violet waters.

"A paintbox morning," Ronnie said, her voice as soft as the surrounding colors. "Isn't it worth getting out of bed for this?"

"A paintbox morning," he echoed, thinking this woman the only person capable of originating such a delightful expression. "Beautiful."

"Feel up to a short walk? Let me help you with your shoes."

She was down on her knees before he realized what she was doing, and he bent to help her to her feet, raising his voice to object. "Veronica—" He caught himself. Sudden movement troubled his injury.

"I don't want you sitting down in this wet sand," she insisted. "Balance yourself on my shoulder and lift your foot." At a glance she could tell this embarrassed him. "Come on, now. When you get better, you can try the glass slipper on my foot."

He smiled as he straightened and gave her one bare foot. "Did you lose a slipper at the dance last night?"

"Come to think of it, I was barefooted. No wonder the prince never comes looking for me."

She brushed her fingers over the bottom of his foot, releasing sand and tingling sensations. Miguel had trouble holding up his end of the conversation. "I'll pack one of your shoes with me when I leave."

She looked up as she guided his foot into a shoe. "You won't have to try it out on too many people. No one else would want to claim my old gym shoes."

His smile broadened. "Especially not from a rebel who was stripped of the rank he never earned and left for dead."

"Some days it just doesn't pay to get up in the morning," she quipped as she finished her task.

He reached for her hand. "This isn't one of them."

They walked hand in hand over the wind-rippled dunes and basked in the rising sun. The cool breeze would soon give way to a warm day full of welcome sunshine. As the sun gained height, the sea turned jade and turquoise, and Miguel thought of the dress Ronnie had worn the previous night. This morning she was back to tan shorts and a shirt she'd left unbuttoned over a salmon-pink top. Her shirt sleeves were rolled above her elbows, and the shirt tails fluttered as she walked beside him. The morning sun danced in her blond hair, glinting red-gold. It was the first time he'd seen her outdoors in the sunlight, and it struck him that the sun might have sired her. It gave her hair its own fire and made her skin honey gold, honey sweet. He noticed the dusting of pale freckles across her nose. There were more of them above the scoop neck of her top, and he imagined them slipping between her breasts.

He scolded himself for creating the image. He'd challenged himself to keep her dressed in his mind, just as she kept herself dressed in his bed—*her* bed. He didn't seem to be up to the challenge. His weakened physical state was, he felt, to blame for all this untempered longing. It seemed that no part of him could escape being touched by this woman's refreshingly unsophisticated beauty.

As they neared a huge, skeletal tree, weathered softly white and standing as a lone sentry on the beach, Miguel shaded his eyes with his free hand. Like the clouds overhead, the white beach now gleamed in the morning sun, and, as much as he loved the sea, such brightness was the bane of Miguel's existence. He felt a tap on his shoulder.

"Would these help?" Ronnie offered the sunglasses she'd bought him. "Just happened to have them in my pocket."

"Gracias, señorita." He smiled as he pushed the black bows through the thick, dark hair at his temples. "You're becoming intimately acquainted with all my weaknesses."

"If that's true, then I can vouch for the fact that you don't have many. It's only been a couple of days since I thought I might have to dig your grave in my backyard." He barked a laugh, enjoying the wonder of his narrow escape now that it was accomplished. "I'm not kidding," Ronnie insisted. "And now look at you. Strolling on the beach just as pretty as you please."

"I'm trying to keep up appearances because I'm with such a pretty girl."

"Time out," she said with a laugh. This man had a way of warming her insides from head to toe. "Time to take a rest. Prop yourself up against old Methuselah here." She indicated the smooth, ashen trunk of the bare-limbed, barkless tree. Its exposed roots undulated in and out of the sand, clutching at barren ground like the bony fingers of a dying man.

Miguel leaned one shoulder against the tree and looked out at the sea. The last time he'd stood this way, there had been a gun at his back. He'd said a quick prayer and prepared himself to die. Now he watched this woman, who'd held his head in her lap and eased his pain, as she walked a few steps away from him to let tongues of sea foam wash her feet. He was grateful to be alive, glad to be here with her, and if he had any sense at all he would stay with her and live to love her. He knew she cared for him.

"Is it cold?" he asked.

"Kind of. And it's usually clearer than this, but the storm churned it up." The water drew back and left a piece of brown sea boa clinging to her toes. She laughed and let the next surge carry the weed away.

"It's good to see the sun again." It sparkled in the water behind her, enhancing her very nature for his enjoyment.

"Even though it hurts your eyes?"

"It doesn't now. I've got my shades." It would hurt more than just his eyes to turn his back on her sunny smile, and he needed to prepare himself for that. Later. He extended his hand. "Come here. I want to tell you something."

She went to him and took his hand as she lifted her chin and let the breeze lift a hank of hair away from her hair. "I'm listening."

"*Bueno*, because I want to tell you how beautiful you look this morning." She smiled. He brought her arm around his waist and held it there while he touched her neck, insinuating his fingertips beneath her shirt collar. "You wear the sea as well as you wore that dress last night. The colors are perfect for you."

"I'm wearing brown shorts and an equally brown shirt." Still she smiled, and the challenge to flatter her more danced in her eyes.

"Immaterial."

"It *is* material. One hundred per cent cotton."

"No, no, *querida*, a moment ago the sea dressed you in aquamarine, the color of your eyes. The most exquisite shade of—"

"You know what I've concluded?" A step closer put her on top of an exposed tree root and brought her eye level near his as she slipped her other arm around his waist.

"What have you concluded?" Now that she had her arms around him of her own accord, he could explore both her shoulders with gently kneading fingers.

"I think it's just the way you talk. Even when you're half out of your mind with pain, you talk like that."

He moved his hands over her neck as though he were molding her out of clay, and he lifted her chin with his thumbs. "Like what?"

"You say pretty things." And she was getting mushy inside. She wished his eyes weren't hidden behind the glasses.

"Pretty things come to mind when I look at you. I need to remember..."

She watched his lips part slightly as he lowered his head.

"Remember." He brushed a kiss against her lips.

"Remember... what?"

"Remember me, *querida*."

He enfolded her in his arms and covered her mouth with his. Her balance on the root was tenuous, and she tried to grip it with her toes, but Miguel slid one arm around her hips and pressed them tight against his. She tried to keep her weight off his injured side, but he seemed unaware of any pain as he urged her mouth open and slipped his tongue inside. Hers greeted his, tentatively at first, then eagerly. When his glasses got in the way, it was Ronnie who took them off.

"Just keep your eyes closed," she murmured against his mouth. With a groan, he slanted his mouth across hers again.

His eyes were still closed when he tipped his head back against the tree and put mind over matter to steady his breathing. She, too, was gathering her wits. He felt her body stiffen as she tried to regain her balance and take care not to lean against his bad side.

"Are you okay, Miguel?"

He turned one corner of his mouth up without opening his eyes. "Are you?"

"Too soon to tell."

"And too late to pretend."

"I think I'm much better than okay."

He looked down at her now, his eyes soft and warm. "I think so, too." He eased her away from him, steadying her as she stepped back from the camel-backed root. Then he moved his thumb slowly over her moist, full lips. "I will remember you, Veronica. Long after you've forgotten me."

Her protest died in her throat, stung by the threat of tears. She gave her head a quick shake, and he tucked her under his arm on his good side and started them on the walk to the house.

"I have to make a phone call." Whoever Miguel was trying to call was a busy man. Miguel left message after message on the answering machine. For two days he watched the phone as though he could make the right call come by sheer concentration, but the only calls came from Barnaby and Becky. Becky had decided to spend a few days with her sister in St. Petersburg and had gotten Barnaby to agree to drive her there. Ronnie recognized the effort for what it was and thanked her friend, assuring her that all was well on their little island. *Everyone* was just fine.

With each call to the answering machine, Miguel's mood seemed to darken. He became more withdrawn, spent more time sitting on the porch, smoking. Conversations were politely strained. He walked the beach late at night, and he made it clear that he preferred to spend the time alone. But when he came to bed, he insisted Ronnie be there. He persisted in holding her, there in the darkness, where he would recite to himself the litany of reasons he had to return to a place where people he loved might shoot him on sight. And there was another list to be etched on the brain—that of reasons to leave the one person he knew he could truly trust.

When the call finally came, Ronnie handed the phone to Miguel and turned to leave the room. But then he called the man by name.

McQuade.

Chapter 7

McQuade!'' Ronnie exclaimed as she edged closer. "Sloan McQuade? The one who—"

"Shh!" Miguel raised a hand for silence. "This is a bad connection. I can't—"

"Where is he? Is he in De Colores? Is Elizabeth Donnelly with him?"

Miguel scowled at Ronnie while he tried to put the pieces together and, at the same time, tried to make himself heard. "McQuade, can you hear me? Yes, Miguel Hidalgo. Yes, yes, the *late* Miguel Hidalgo. Cancel your order for funeral flowers, McQuade. No. As it turns out, my executioners were poor marksmen."

Miguel found it hard to laugh at McQuade's response and shake Ronnie off his arm at the same time.

"Where are they, Miguel?" she asked. "Is Elizabeth with him? Find out if Elizabeth is with him."

"Elizabeth?" Miguel was having trouble deciding which way to direct his conversation. "Is Elizabeth with you?"

Ronnie watched the light dawn in Miguel's eyes as he listened to the voice on the other end of the line. It looked good. She held her tongue and crossed her fingers, but from the look on Miguel's face, Elizabeth was safe.

"I think I may be able to answer that for you, McQuade." Miguel surveyed Ronnie up and down, his eyes dancing. "Was your pilot a little over five feet tall, reddish-blond hair, blue-green eyes, usually wears— Yes, that's the one. I'm looking at her. I'm afraid I hijacked your rescue plane, my friend." McQuade's response brought another laugh. "I'm not familiar with that expression, McQuade. I'll have to brush up on your American street language. However, I'm alive and very nearly well in the Florida Keys, and you and Elizabeth are safe in Arco Iris. How long will you be there?"

"Did Elizabeth get her baby?" Ronnie demanded in a stage whisper.

Miguel nodded and gestured for her to hold her questions for just another moment. "I want you to help me get back to De Colores," he told McQuade. "No, but I'll find a way. Yes, as soon as I can." Miguel laughed. "Not to give *them* another shot. I was thinking of returning fire. You, too? I'm afraid you'll have to stand in line, amigo. Yes, I'll be in touch."

Miguel hung up the phone, and he and Ronnie stood looking at one another for a moment, sorting through the pieces of news. "Your passengers are safe," he said, almost reverently. "They got away on a fishing boat after the hurricane. Elizabeth is free of Guerrero, and she has her son."

"I didn't really know all the details. I take it Guerrero is the child's father."

Miguel smiled as he put his image of hard-shelled McQuade together with the way the man had just spoken of Elizabeth. "I suspect the boy will soon have a new father."

"McQuade?"

"McQuade."

Again they looked at one another, and their smiles faded.

"And so you're leaving."

"I'll meet McQuade in Arco Iris, and from there—"

"Arco Iris is no problem."

His eyes became stony. "No, Veronica."

"Listen, I can take you that far. There's no risk—"

The touch of her hand was the problem. The risk lay in the way it made him feel. "No. It ends here."

"What ends?" She gripped both his arms now and felt her pride drain away as she looked up at him. "There's nothing to end, Miguel. Nothing ever got started. We shared a bed, but not . . . it was just . . ."

"Just what?"

"Just one of those things, as the song says." She cast around for words, wanting to tell him what it really was for her while she still had the chance. But she knew if she did, she would get nowhere with her offer. "Just a sweet interlude. Like something out of a movie." His dark eyes softened, and he brought his hands up slowly and curved them around her back, but he said nothing. "And no one got hurt," she added quietly. "So it's okay. There's no reason you shouldn't fly with me. There's no—"

His kiss unleashed the need he'd felt for days. He'd longed to fly with her, bury himself deep inside her and soar on and on with her. He plunged his tongue into the soft, wet warmth of her mouth, slid his hand to her hip and pressed her firmly against him, trying to content himself with a semblance of what he wanted. It was like trying to satisfy a terrible hunger with just the aroma of a delicious meal. He ended the kiss as abruptly as he had begun. She laid her head against his shoulder, and they stood together, holding one another close enough to share a heartbeat. For the hundredth time he entertained the thought of not going back. For the hundredth time he damned himself for a self-serving coward. He had to make a move, or he would lose his mind.

"How soon can you have your plane ready?" he asked finally.

Arco Iris was a bright little island whose population seemed to thrive on the business of enjoying life. The island shared De Colores's fishing waters but not her political problems. Because Arco Iris was Mexican territory, Miguel felt reasonably safe as he and

Ronnie left the green and white Cessna at the airstrip and headed for the Oyster Shell, McQuade's favorite guest house on the island.

Felix Santiago made a habit of greeting every guest under the ever-creaking paddle fan in the rattan and potted-palm appointed lobby of the Oyster Shell, and he never forgot a face. The little blonde had checked in a couple of weeks ago with McQuade. As Felix recalled, she had flown McQuade in with Elizabeth Donnelly. He could have sworn he knew the man with her, too. Even behind the dark glasses and looking a bit leaner than he remembered, Felix was certain he knew this man. Of course, Miguel Hidalgo was dead, but the resemblance was remarkable.

"Two rooms, *por favor*," the man said.

Felix turned to Ronnie, who doffed her red baseball cap and shook out a profusion of strawberry-blond hair. "So you brought me another guest, Miss Harper. McQuade and his lady returned, you know, with the little boy. I think McQuade is—" he raised his eyebrows and gave a conspiratorial smile as he pushed registration forms across the desk "—headed for the altar straightaway."

Miguel picked up a pen and began filling out a form. "We'd like to see McQuade right away," Ronnie told Felix. "He's expecting us."

Felix raked his fingers through his slick black hair and abandoned any pretense of subtlety by twisting his head to look at the name of Miguel's registration form. "Is McQuade a friend of yours, too, Señor... Fortuna?"

"Yes, he is."

"Where are you from, señor? If I may ask."

"Miami." Miguel took the key from Felix's hand and picked up their two small bags. "Which room is McQuade's?"

"I can call him, señor, just…" The man behind the sunglasses did not wish to wait. "Room nine. Please tell us if there's anything…" Miguel was on his way up the stairs. Felix handed Ronnie the second key. "Anything you need. He is a *friend*, you say?"

"Yes, very definitely."

By the time Ronnie stepped around the smooth curve of the mahogany banister at the top of the stairs, Miguel was already embracing the beautiful Elizabeth Donnelly with one arm and shaking hands with McQuade with the other. A dark-eyed toddler rode contentedly in the arm of the big, blond private investigator, whom Ronnie never would have imagined to look so natural carrying a child. She stood hesitantly on the landing, thinking the scene seemed quite complete without her. She would have been satisfied to sneak right past without having to answer to McQuade at all.

"Would you look at this," McQuade announced. "Amelia Earhart returns. I think you oughta hire a new navigator, sweetheart."

"I'm really sorry, McQuade." Ronnie rubbed her palm over the polished wooden handrail. "There were these two guys with guns, and Miguel was bleeding all over the place. I tried to get back, but—"

"For what it's worth, this woman saved my life. Inadvertently, you two arranged for my rescue." Miguel stepped away from the couple and held his hand out to invite Ronnie to join them.

She accepted it, grateful for any moral support. She still had the feeling that somehow she could have been in two places at once, and that any excuse for her failure would sound lame. "I had engine trouble, and then the storm hit."

"Thank God you were able to help Miguel, Ronnie," Elizabeth said, and smiled. "Your untimely departure gave Sloan a chance to earn his outrageous fee."

"Yeah, well—" McQuade hooked his free arm around Elizabeth's shoulders and pulled her against him. "What with compound interest, it'll take you a lifetime to pay up, lady." They exchanged a secret promise as Elizabeth turned to look at him. "Did you guys get rooms?" McQuade finally thought to ask.

The answers came quickly, simultaneously.

"Yes."

"Yes, we did."

McQuade laughed. He remembered when intimate looks between people in love had made him edgy, too. Weeks ago, in another life. "Why don't you settle in, get cleaned up, and then we'll trade hurricane stories over dinner."

Miguel's room was right next door to Ronnie's, and she knew that the extra door joined them. The security chain dangled near the door frame. She started to fasten it, then changed her mind and let it drop. She didn't have to lock him out. She didn't want to. But they weren't alone together in her little world anymore, and there was no longer any excuse for them to share intimate space, to come and go as though their lives were one. Miguel would be resting in the other room. It had been a long day, and he'd looked tired. He had his bed, and she had hers.

Ronnie opened her bag and began unpacking toiletries and the few articles of clothing she'd brought. In a little while they'd go downstairs to the dining room, and there would be women wearing summer dresses having dinner with the men who admired them. She came to the bottom of the bag and knew even as she reached for it that she was being silly. The sea-foam dress, Miguel had called it. She lifted it high, shook it out and then held it up to her shoulders as she turned toward the mirror. She could afford to buy dresses. She just didn't. Oh, she had a couple of skirts in her closet for emergencies, but her life didn't call for dresses. This one was so outdated. Not that she knew that much about styles, but it had to be. She thought of the pretty yellow sundress Elizabeth had been wearing, and the warm way McQuade had looked at her. Elizabeth would look elegant in a flour sack, but not Ronnie. Ronnie could put on some high-fashion designer outfit, and she knew she'd still look like one of the guys.

She folded the dress and put it back in the bottom of the bag. This was an island resort, and her casual clothes were perfectly acceptable. She'd feel ridiculous trying to be someone she wasn't, especially in front of Elizabeth and McQuade. In private it had been one thing, but she wasn't about to take such a risk in public. Miguel would probably be embarrassed for her.

Miguel stood by the open window in his room and watched the sun sink toward the sea. He took a long, slow drag on his cigarette and blew the smoke away, watching it dissipate in the clear evening air. He had managed to pry McQuade away from Elizabeth long enough to enlist his help in finding transportation to De Colores. McQuade had made several contacts, and, with any luck, Miguel could be gone by morning.

Luck. He'd called himself Fortuna, which was a strange choice, indeed. He'd never believed in luck. He believed in reason. He believed that right would prevail because it was reasonable, and he could take that belief one step further to explain why his body hadn't been carried away by the tide. Raphael and Paulo had carried him from the beach because it was the right and rational thing to do. He wasn't alive because of luck. It was not reasonable for Guerrero to kill him. Guerrero's power on the island was an insult to reason. The only reasonable course of action for Miguel was to return and seek out the *reasonable* people, who would undoubtedly support him.

Miguel stuck the cigarette into the corner of his mouth and began unbuttoning his shirt. He was satisfied that he had it all figured out until he brushed his hand against the square bandage that was taped to his side—the bandage Veronica had put there that morning. Veronica defied reason, and calling her a stroke of luck would not fit her into a comfortable niche in his brain.

She had not happened along by chance. She had come to De Colores with a purpose, and he had spirited her away at gunpoint. But he'd been too weak to force her to make any further decisions. She'd made them all on her own, and, in view of the fact that he had diverted her from her purpose by force, none of her decisions had been reasonable. She had helped him. She had protected him from her own father. And she had brought him here. In all these things, she'd been motivated by kindness, not by reason. He plucked the cigarette from his mouth and smiled. His angel had a great capacity for kindness and, yes, for love. He believed in that, too. He also believed it would be a mistake for her to love Miguel Hidalgo right now. She was bound to make more unreasonable choices—choices that would be dangerous for her. And each time he held her in his arms, he felt his own reasonable resolve slip another notch. For her sake, he *had* to be gone by morning.

She'd been ready for some time when he knocked at the door. She looked so pretty that he thought he would have to launch a steady barrage of flowery compliments just to keep his mouth busy. He wanted to kiss her.

"How pretty you look."

"I suppose I could go out tomorrow and look for some sort of dress," she said as she glanced at herself in the mirror. She'd sent her tan slacks and her yellow and white striped shirt out to be pressed, and they looked crisp and neat. She'd washed her hair and made an attempt to fluff it up with a brush and a blow drier. She'd even used a little mascara on her nearly non-existent lashes. "You know, for dinner. With the four of us together, people will sort of think that I'm with you, and I didn't bring much to wear." She looked up at him as though she'd just stepped on his toe. "I thought I'd stay around for a few days and see that you, um—don't try to rush your convalescence."

"I didn't bring much to wear, either," he reminded her. "If blue jeans are prohibited in the dining room, I'm out of luck."

"I wore shorts the last time I was here." She wanted to tell him how wonderful he looked in his jeans, but instead she said, "I'm sorry. I should have gotten you some slacks. You're probably used to wearing—"

"I'm used to wearing a uniform, which never fit me. I can hardly remember what I wore before that." He smiled and offered his arm. "If you have no objections to dining with a man in blue jeans..."

Her smile made her face glow as she slipped her hand into the crook of his arm. "Actually, I kind of like the idea."

Elizabeth and McQuade had already been seated at a table for four. Ronnie had been certain that no one looked more beautiful than Elizabeth Donnelly with her black hair cascading past her shoulders, but now she decided she had been wrong. Elizabeth Donnelly with her hair in an elegant twist was equally beautiful. The same yellow sundress took on a whole new look, and Ronnie couldn't wait to hide her own slacks beneath the tablecloth.

"Where's the baby?" Miguel asked as he held Ronnie's chair for her.

"One of Felix's many cousins is sitting with Tomas tonight," Elizabeth said.

"We spent most of the day splashing in the surf," McQuade added. "I had him doing a pretty respectable dog paddle already. Wore the little guy out."

"Tomas tags after Sloan like a little tail." Elizabeth gave the image some thought and added with a laugh, "A tail that wags the dog. We're going to have quite a job unspoiling him once we get back to Miami."

McQuade saw the anticipatory gleam in their friends' eyes. "The woman has no choice but to marry me," he explained. "Gotta keep the tail and the dog together."

It was clear that Elizabeth had chosen a man who loved her this time. Ronnie remembered the sad, haunted woman who'd chartered her plane. Elizabeth deserved this happiness, and, from what Ronnie had heard of the difficulties she and McQuade had overcome to recover little Tomas, she had paid dearly for it. The stories the couple told filled Ronnie's mind with one thought: in a matter of days Miguel would be in the very trouble spot these two had left behind.

"How bad is the damage?" Miguel asked. He turned the stem of a goblet between his thumb and forefinger and watched the red liquid slosh in the glass.

McQuade sighed, laid his fork on his plate and looked up at Miguel. "It's bad, amigo. Villages went down like dominoes. Fishing boats were smashed in their moorings, trees beaten to the ground. I didn't have time to take any inventories, but I saw some pretty battered cane fields."

"Guerrero will ask other governments for aid." Miguel sipped the wine and then pressed his lips together, appreciating the bitter aftertaste. "If he gets it, very little will reach the people."

"He seems to have a penchant for military toys," McQuade said.

Elizabeth grew impatient with the way the conversation seemed to skirt the immediate issues. "There are soldiers everywhere. I know what you have in mind, but if you go back there now . . . Miguel, if you fall into his hands, he'll see you dead himself this time, and he'll take pleasure in it."

"I am inspired by your own act of courage, Elizabeth." The fierce look in her eyes brought a mirthless smile to his lips. She, too, had come to know Guerrero the hard way.

He did not doubt the quick tempered dictator had been a cruel husband. "I'm going to find out how many others in De Colores have the same kind of courage. Even while I devoted my attention to what I considered to be the real needs of the people, I was not completely out of touch with Guerrero's little army. They follow him out of fear.''

"I can understand that," Elizabeth said quietly.

"But Veronica can vouch for the fact that I have at least two loyal followers."

Ronnie turned at the sound of her name and basked in his warm smile, which she took to be a gentle apology for having held her at gunpoint. "You left two loyal followers behind. I hope they're still there."

"They're waiting for me, and there will be others. It's partly because of my own stupidity that Guerrero has come this far. But he can be stopped. His ludicrous ego is a fatal weakness."

"The people you're counting on to help you are in desperate need of supplies right about now," McQuade pointed out. "The way he's got transportation sewed up, you're gonna have a hell of a time—"

"But I brought transportation." Ronnie was suddenly the center of attention, and she had the feeling she'd said the wrong thing. Even Elizabeth's expression indicated disapproval. Ronnie straightened her back and squared her shoulders. "Now, look, I've been flying Red Cross supplies for years. If they can get me clearance, there's no reason I couldn't smuggle a few—"

McQuade dismissed the notion lightly. "Don't even think it, kid. If I'd known what was waiting for us on that island, I'd have locked Elizabeth up someplace in Miami."

"And I'd have cursed you until your dying day."

"Aw, c'mon, honey." McQuade covered Elizabeth's hand with his. "You'd have changed your tune when I brought Tomas back to you."

Their contentment made Ronnie squirm. Their ordeal was over now, and they could afford to look back and say they would have taken fewer chances. But Miguel was climbing into the crater of a seething volcano, and Ronnie had only one practical kind of help to offer him. She didn't want to tip her hand entirely, so she searched for a casual response.

"Listen, you guys, I'm not just another pretty face. I'm a pilot. I do this for a living."

"Smuggling?" McQuade laughed. "You're as wholesome as your orange juice, Ronnie." He nodded toward her glass. "Drink up."

Without touching her, Miguel sensed the stiffness in her body. McQuade was unaware that he'd thrown a gauntlet at her feet. Her suggestion was not to be dismissed with a joke. "We'll talk about it later, Veronica. In fact—" he managed his most charming smile for the entire table's benefit "—I suggest we turn our conversation to more pleasant matters. This talk of a wedding, for example." He lifted his glass. "I hope I'm not too late to offer the very first congratulatory toast."

Discussion of her plan was not the only motive Miguel had for asking Ronnie to walk with him on the beach. There was the waxing moon in a sky hung generously with stars, and there were his needs—the need to be alone with her on this last night and the need to avoid the door between their rooms, the one he knew she hadn't locked. And there was the very practical need to see that she stayed awake most of the night so that she would sleep in the morning.

They had rolled up the bottoms of their pants and left their shoes behind. Small waves broke gently and lapped the sand, now washing their feet, now sliding away. Miguel slipped his arm around Ronnie's shoulders. "Do you mind if we walk like lovers?"

She put her arm around his waist. "It seems the thing to do on a night like this."

"In another world—another time and place—we would have shared more."

"Had you stayed a college professor, you never would have met me," she pointed out.

"I might have chartered your plane for an expedition. Research on the Aztec ruins in the islands of the Caribbean."

She slid a glance up at him. "Are there any?"

He smiled as he promised, "We would have left no stone unturned in our search for them."

"Really? Would you have taken the summer off?"

"I would have taken a year's sabbatical."

"Just to look for ruins?"

He stopped and turned her into his arms. "Just to fly with you," he said, and then he kissed the salt spray from her lips. He found her own delicious taste underneath, and pried her lips apart with his tongue, savoring it like a child seldom treated to candy. *"Muy dulce,"* he muttered. "Sweet, so sweet."

Ronnie curled her toes in the wet sand and pressed her palms against his back. He was so much taller than she was, even when she dug in and stood on tiptoe, that she had to tip her head back and let his kisses come to her. And they came, filled her mouth, filled her heart and made every part of her that touched him ache in sympathy with the need she felt deep, deep down. She felt the cool breeze on her arms, cold water on the bottoms of her feet and the warmth of his breath against her cheek.

"We could fly so much higher," he whispered. He nuzzled her ear and kissed her neck.

She opened her eyes, saw the white moon hanging just above his shoulder and gave a husky chuckle. "You have a good pilot at your disposal, Miguel."

"Mmm, yes." He nudged her collar aside with his nose and tasted her shoulder with the tip of his tongue. "I could take you anywhere you wanted to go."

He lifted his head slowly, cherishing the offer. Her face was brightly moonlit, and he hoped his was sufficiently shadowed. "I don't want to leave, Veronica. If I could choose..." He shook his head, warding off any alternatives. "I have to go back, and I don't know how long it will take...to do what must be done."

"I'm going to get in touch with the Red Cross tomorrow."

"Why?"

He'd gripped her shoulders suddenly and assumed a wide-legged stance.

"Why not?" She clutched his arms, wishing she had the power to shake some sense into him. "The Red

Cross will tell me exactly what they need, and they'll get me government clearance. It sounds as though food and medical supplies should come first. I'm sure you've talked to McQuade about guns. Once I've made a few routine deliveries, I should be able to—"

"No!" Miguel didn't believe what he was hearing. He'd anticipated her persistence in trying to help him get back, or perhaps trying to dissuade him from going back at all, but this plan was suicidal. Gunrunning!

"Miguel, I am a charter pilot. I've been making regular deliveries—"

"Contraband?"

"What?"

"Have you been delivering contraband, Veronica?"

"Of course not!"

He slid his hands to her upper arms and gentled his voice. "That's what you're suggesting now. Delivering guns to an outlaw."

"You're not an outlaw," she insisted. "By all rights you should be the law in De Colores."

"Soon after I return from the grave, I will be declared an outlaw, and anyone who aids me—" his voice grew softer "—comforts me—" and softer still "—consorts with me...Veronica, you saved my life. I will not have you die for me."

"I won't." She saw the gleam in his eyes, and her throat went dry. "I won't die. I'll be...careful."

"As you were on your last trip to the island?" He laughed and pulled her against his chest. "*I'll* be careful. I won't let you get mixed up in this."

How could he stop her? She'd never been mixed up in anything more deeply than she was with this man's life. She tucked in her chin and pressed her forehead against a button on his shirt. "Are we going to make love before you leave, Miguel?" He took a slow, deep breath, and her head rose and fell with his chest. No answer came. She leaned back and looked at him. "Before you go off to start your revolution, will we..." She bit off the words. "Maybe we could save this argument for another time and just...walk along the beach like lovers."

He put his arm around her again, and they walked without talking and let the water wash their feet.

And later, when it was almost time, Miguel slipped through the door that separated their rooms. She slept bathed in moonlight, the picture of the angel he knew her to be. Her head was pillowed on her arm, and her lips looked moist, as though he'd just kissed them. He wanted her to know how much he loved her, but nothing would stop her from following him then. His love would lead her into a hotbed of danger. He couldn't trade her safety for the ecstasy of making her truly his. She still had choices. For him, there was none. But if he could have chosen, made one claim, allowed himself one personal concession, it would have been Veronica.

Chapter 8

Raphael recognized the green and white airplane. Its wheels skimmed the cracking surface of the old airstrip without a bounce. He motioned for the men in his party to meet the craft on the field, but he reached for Paulo's shoulder and pulled him back before he could step away from the trees with the rest. "It's the *gringa*—the one who took the *jefe* to the States. He'll want to know she's here."

Paulo nodded and trotted off toward the village. He cradled the .22-caliber rifle as though it were an M-16. The next automatic rifle they got hold of would go to Paulo, Raphael vowed as he turned back to deal with the visitor from the north. Miguel had said nothing to Raphael about sending for the woman, but she'd flown in like she owned the place. In the three weeks since his return to De Colores, the *jefe* had said little about the time he'd spent away except that the woman had kept his confidence and seen to his recovery. But somehow she must have known that Miguel and his followers held the villages in this area, including El Gallo and this airstrip. Otherwise she surely would not have risked such a bold landing.

Miguel took a two-fisted hold on the canvas tent he'd been helping to repair and came to his feet slowly as the news sank in. He'd ignored the sound of engines in the air, assuming that, as usual, the plane was headed for La Primavera. "You've *seen* her, Paulo?"

"I couldn't see the pilot, but it's her plane. I remember the numbers on it," Paulo announced, hoping his astuteness would not go unnoticed. "Shall I drive you to the airfield, *jefe*?"

Miguel paused a moment to hand his side of the tent back to the young couple who owned it. The thought of her being there unnerved him, and he needed time to overcome his weakness. He turned to Paulo, who waited so anxiously to do his bidding. "Have her move the plane into the trees at the east end of the field," Miguel said finally. "Tell Raphael to camouflage it thoroughly. You are to bring *Señorita* Harper directly to my quarters."

"Yes, sir. Do you want me to tell her anything?"

"That she's up to her neck in hot water." Seeing the surprise in Paulo's big brown eyes, he laughed and shook his head. "No, just tell her you're bringing her to see me."

"Yes, sir." Paulo turned to leave.

"Take the jeep, Paulo. Show her we've got class."

Paulo grinned. "Yes, sir."

Class was not a scale-tripping advantage when they were up against superior firepower, but women liked it. Miguel realized the implications of that thought as soon as he'd formulated it, and he dismissed Paulo with a more impatient gesture than he'd intended. Was he actually entertaining thoughts of impressing this woman when she had absolutely no business being here? He turned on his heel and strode toward the far end of the gravel street and the metal Quonset building, which served as a supply depot and his private quarters.

Ignoring a greeting from the crew assigned to salvage anything useful from the wreckage left behind by the hurricane, Miguel noted three more tents standing in one of the temporary camps. They meant either more recruits or more refugee families. Either way, there would be more mouths to feed.

He waited beneath the thatched shelter he'd built near the Quonset. Overturned crates provided seating, and a patch of dirt served as the drawing board for his strategy sessions. He remembered the massive mahogany desk in the office he had occupied in the east wing of the presidential palace, and realized that he liked this office better. It had no walls. From here he could see how his people fared. He picked up a stick and scratched the letter *V* in the dirt. For victory? Or for Veronica? At the sound of the jeep's roaring engine, he reached down and erased the evidence of his yearnings.

The red baseball cap proclaimed her identity. Surrounded by dark-haired, brown-skinned young men armed with various forms of weaponry, she bounced in the seat next to Paulo with only the cap occasionally rising above the top of the windshield. Miguel regretted the fuel he'd expended in this show of hospitality as he watched them approach. Raphael and Paulo escorted her to the shelter as though she had been granted an audience with a man of real power. For the sake of their morale, he allowed them that fancy. Their rebel band now had squads and committees, details and inspections. He claimed leadership, but he refused to claim rank.

"*Señorita* Harper's plane is loaded with medical and food supplies," Raphael announced as he ducked from the sunlight into the shade of dried palm thatching. "With your permission, we will transfer everything to Supply."

Miguel nodded, concentrating on Raphael's face and avoiding Ronnie's. What he could see of her in the periphery was enough to make his throat go dry. "Use Antonio's truck," he ordered. Even though the people of the village had generously made their property available for the good of the cause, Miguel insisted upon acknowledging private ownership. Guerrero had dealt with disaster by laying claim to anything he could use after the hurricane, and the people, already disgruntled, had finally begun to balk.

"No need to worry about gas," Paulo said proudly. "After I picked up the first watch and dropped off their replacements last night, we appropriated a full tank from one of the so-called People's gas pumps.''

Miguel's scowl skittered past Ronnie as he turned to Paulo and demanded, ''On whose authority?''

''On...well, I—'' the boy shrugged, and his face fell ''—thought we needed gas.''

''Raphael, take this boy with you, and explain to him why we don't make raids on a whim.''

''Yes, sir,'' Raphael replied, whacking Paulo's arm with the back of his hand as he backed into the sunlight again.

''Not even on the *People's* gas pumps, Paulo.''

''Yes, sir,'' came the retreating, disappointed response.

Ronnie stood quietly under the rustling thatch and waited for Miguel to really look at her. She knew he was putting it off as long as he could. He watched the two young men spar with one another as they returned to the jeep and shook his head, speaking to himself rather than to her. ''They ask for permission to unload supplies, but they wander beyond our lines on the spur of the moment to steal a tank of gas.''

Wordlessly she watched him rake his fingers through his thick, black hair. She wondered whether his jeans were the ones she'd bought for him. If they were, he'd lost weight. His face, though more deeply tanned, looked drawn, angular. He finally turned to her, and he was able to maintain a hard, forbidding stare for a moment. His look challenged her to offer an excuse for being there, one that he could cut to shreds with imperious logic. But she said nothing, because excuses and reasons would add up to a lot of hot air. She was there, and that was that.

His dark eyes softened, and he almost chuckled, *almost* smiled. "And what am I supposed to do with you?" he asked finally.

"Nothing," she said quietly. "You're supposed to take the supplies I brought and put them to good use."

Her eyes were as stirring as he remembered, those cool facets of aquamarine drawing him closer, offering respite from all his cares. All but one. They refused to release him from the one that made the syllables of her name an integral part of his heartbeat. Supplies, he reminded himself. "You didn't bring any guns, did you?"

"No, I'm sorry. I didn't."

"I'm sorry, too, that you didn't." He saw a flicker of surprise in her eyes. She swallowed quickly, absently pressed her lips together to moisten them and waited. What was she waiting for? The question was foolish; he knew the answer well. He felt the same tingling on his own lips and longed for the same taste. He watched a trickle of perspiration follow the snaky path of a tendril of copper-yellow hair that was plastered to the edge of her face and smiled. "On the other hand, if you had flown in here carrying guns, I would have been furious with you."

"Does that mean that you're not?" she asked hopefully.

"It means that I need guns as much as I need fuel. But you are just as reckless as Paulo is. I should paddle you both."

"Before you even say hello?"

He lifted his gaze to the scene behind her. What had once been a sleepy fishing village was now an armed camp, and everything that happened here was his business. Raphael had taken the jeep across the street to the little gas station, now the motor pool, where tavern owner Antonio Moreno had recently been made quartermaster. Antonio's beloved twenty-year-old daughter, Chi Chi, had one eye on Raphael's squad and the other on Miguel's conversation with the bold and obviously female Anglo pilot. Nothing Miguel did escaped his people's notice. The only thing they could not see was the way his palms tingled with the thought of greeting this woman properly.

"Hello, Veronica."

The flash of disappointment in her eyes pierced a soft place inside him. Without explanation, he took her by the arm, led her to a door at the back of the Quonset and ushered her inside. He lifted the cap from her head and released her hair. It was damp and replete with her special brand of lemon scent. The cap fell to the floor as Miguel placed the tips of his fingers at her temples and moved his hands slowly, letting the silken strands slide through his fingers while she watched his eyes fill up with pleasure. Suddenly, swiftly, he took her in his arms and said hello again, this time with an urgent kiss. Ronnie felt a flood of relief pour over her, which manifested itself in an unusual, unexpected trickle of tears from the corners of her eyes. She parted her lips to touch his tongue with hers and greet him. He hadn't forgotten her!

Her hand skated over his back to the place she'd tended, and she felt the puckered flesh through his shirt. When he lifted his head, she caught her breath, then asked, "How are you, Miguel? Are you okay?"

"I'm healing very well, thank you." He brushed the track of her tear from her temple. "What's the matter, *querida*?"

"You're not angry." Her voice went husky on the last word.

With a brief kiss he took away the tears from the other side of her face and whispered, "Of course I am."

"It doesn't show."

He chuckled. "Are you disappointed?"

"Relieved," she said with a sigh. "Very relieved, and very, very glad to see you."

"You shouldn't be here, and I am *not* pleased to see you here." He pressed a kiss into her hair and hugged her possessively. "But it pleases me to hold you, *mi angel*."

"Oh, Miguel, I had to come. The news releases about you are so confusing."

"Nobody's asked me for an interview." He laughed, but when he leaned back to look at her he saw that she didn't share his amusement. "Our numbers are growing, and we're just beginning to pose a threat. Have we made network news?"

"They're not sure what to make of you. One day they say you're reported to be leading a rebellion against the Guerrero regime, and the next day the uprising is under control, and there are rumors of your arrest." She looked up at him and touched his face as if to convince herself that his flesh was warm. "Once they reported that your body had been discovered in the—" With a quick shake of her head, she dismissed the terrible vision. "But later they identified it as someone else."

She'd grieved for him. In her eyes he saw the remembered pain, and he touched her neck with gentle fingers and traced the line of her jaw with his thumb. "I'm sorry."

"They say you're hiding in the mountains and terrorizing the villages."

"We've liberated several villages, inviting anyone willing to fight to come and join us," he explained. "We've had a few hit-and-run skirmishes with government troops, but they aren't pressing us. Guerrero stands to lose even more men to desertion if he mounts an attack on these villagers. He's experimenting with propaganda at the moment."

Ronnie slid her hands to his waist. "And are you experimenting with starvation? You look as though you haven't slept or eaten a decent meal in three weeks."

"No one here is eating well."

"I know," she said. "I did get in touch with the Red Cross. And I did get someone to fly supplies into La Primavera for them, but I knew that wouldn't help you. McQuade found out that you had control of this area through his—" she waved her hand "—inexhaustible sources."

"Where is McQuade?"

Ronnie checked her watch. "I'd say he should be coming home to his wife right about now."

Miguel smiled. "They wasted no time, then."

"Neither did you." He looked puzzled. "Leaving Arco Iris, I mean."

He sighed and turned away. The room was too hot. He opened the door and leaned against the door frame. The building stood on a low bluff. Beyond it he could see the small, turquoise lagoon, and beyond that, the blue sea. "I thought it would be easier that way, Veronica."

"Easier for whom?" She found herself speaking to his back.

"For both of us."

"And was it?"

How could he answer that? The bittersweet taste of her kiss lingered on his lips, and he couldn't say whether it was worse to be with her, knowing it couldn't last, or not to be able to see her at all. "I haven't stopped thinking of you," he confessed quietly.

How did he think of her? she wondered. With gratitude? With amusement? Perhaps fondly. "At least you knew I was safe."

"I prayed that you were." He felt her close behind him and wished that she would touch him. "You *will* be safe, Veronica. As soon as the plane is unloaded, you'll be on your way."

"If you're so anxious to give me orders, Miguel, why don't you let me join you? I'm willing to fight. You said—"

"I said nothing about you!" He stepped over the threshold and into the sunlight, struggling to control the tone of his voice as he turned to face her. "Nor anyone who cannot call this island *home*. It is for *us* to fight for our freedom, Veronica. You have no part in this."

Rejection had a razor's edge. *You're* my part in this, she shouted, but only inside her head. She gripped the door frame and sought an impassive comeback. "Would you let McQuade help you?"

He sighed and shoved his hands into the pockets of his jeans. "You must know that I've asked for his help."

"I know that he met Mikal Romanov in Washington, and that Mikal is still there, on your behalf, I assume."

"I hope so," Miguel said. "But it won't do any good until we prove ourselves a force to be reckoned with. In order to do that, we must have—"

"Guns."

"That's right."

"Did you ask McQuade to get them for you?"

"No." He looked away and added quietly, "Not yet. I gave him my power of attorney so that he would have access to what money I have, but to ask him to arrange something that risky..." Miguel shook his head.

"You won't have to ask him. This is Elizabeth's home, too, Miguel. When I tell them what the situation is here—what I've seen—"

"You'll do that?"

"Yes, of course." She stepped closer to him and laid her hand on his arm. "Let's dispel the rumors, Miguel. I brought a video camera. Let's give Mikal Romanov something to work with, and let's let McQuade do what he does best."

Ronnie sat in the McQuades' darkened living room and watched Miguel on the television screen. She had never used a video camera before, and she was making mental notes of all the mistakes she'd made. McQuade seemed impressed. "This is great," he kept mumbling. "You could do this for a living, Ronnie."

"We wanted to show the people—there's Paulo, the one who hijacked me—and the destruction caused by the hurricane. See how Miguel's got everything organized? That's the motor pool."

"There's the cantina," Elizabeth said, pointing to the screen. "That's where I was attacked by that terrible spider."

"Oh, God, there's Chi Chi," McQuade groaned, sinking lower in his chair.

"McQuade! Man of my dreams." Elizabeth's apt mimicry of the flirtatious Chi Chi brought a sheepish grin to her new husband's face.

"This woman has a real jealous streak, I'll tell ya." He leaned forward, bracing his elbows on his knees, and listened more intently as Miguel recounted the attempt on his life and described his efforts to help the people gain their freedom. He explained that there was a shortage of supplies but no shortage of determination. He said that he was not asking anyone to intervene. He believed this was their fight, but he wanted the cause to be understood for what it was. The real terrorist, he said, was in the presidential palace, and the people would not allow Guerrero to stay there much longer.

McQuade moved from his chair to comfort Elizabeth on the sofa, and Ronnie saw that tears had prompted his attentiveness. Elizabeth buried her face in McQuade's shoulder, and he held her as he looked at Ronnie. "We'll express the tape up to Mike Romanov first thing in the morning."

"McQuade, he needs help now," Ronnie said. "Guerrero could decide to attack them any time, and they've got practically nothing to fight back with."

"I know. Elizabeth and I have talked it over, and we agree—" Elizabeth raised her head and took a swipe at her tears with the back of her hand as they exchanged a look. "Well, we're damn near in agreement," McQuade amended with half a smile. "She's staying here with Tomas, and I'm going to Arco Iris to take delivery on a shipment of the, uh, necessary hardware just as soon as I can solve the problem of—"

Elizabeth's pointed glare came too late. Ronnie was ready with, "Transportation?"

From the air De Colores looked like a peaceful little chunk of paradise, but McQuade knew better. Ronnie's skillful approach took them over the mountains and clipped the tops of the trees in an abrupt descent as she flew over what she hoped was still

Miguel's airspace. When they drew fire from the ground, she knew some of it must be under dispute.

"Did they hit anything?" she asked.

McQuade tucked in his chin and looked himself over. "Nothing important on this side. You?"

"I'm fine. Are you sure Miguel's still in control of this field?"

"According to my sources he is, but it looks like somebody's playing a little king-of-the-road back there."

They touched down and taxied toward the east end of the field, where Ronnie had hidden the plane in the trees during her last visit. McQuade reached behind his seat and made contact with the steel barrel of his automatic rifle. He'd been here before, and the air felt just as sticky as ever.

"I'm sure they must have seen us," Ronnie said, scanning the trees.

"Somebody sure as hell saw us," McQuade grumbled as he checked what he knew to be a fully loaded magazine. He shoved it back in place and nodded toward the door. "We're gonna blow this crop duster and find out what we're up against here."

"There's Miguel!"

Leading a squad of men, Miguel strode out of the shadows and cut across the corner of the airstrip. Ronnie and McQuade climbed down and met the welcoming party beside the Cessna's tail.

"I should improvise a jail and arrest you for your stupidity, McQuade." Behind his dark glasses Miguel

could have been one of the faces on Mount Rush-
more.

"Don't use Antonio's back room unless you have it
exterminated first." McQuade found himself laughing solo. "It's, uh . . . it's full of spiders, you know.
Spiders?" No one was paying any attention to him,
and he wasn't quite sure how to interpret the heated
looks Ronnie and Miguel were exchanging. "Look,
Miguel, she's been running back and forth here come
hell or high water for a long time now. It doesn't matter what you say, what I say . . . You sent her after
guns—she brought you guns."

Miguel shifted his cool stare. "I sent her to you,
McQuade. You were supposed to bring the guns."

"In what? My little red wagon? She's been here
twice in the last—"

Ronnie stuck her hands on her hips. "*She* is not out
in the kitchen making coffee while you two discuss *her*
air-charter business. I do this for a living, you know."

Miguel spoke through clenched teeth. "You do not
smuggle arms for—"

"I do now." She shoved the key to the cargo bay
under Miguel's nose. "This is not a gift horse you're
looking in the mouth. You can pay me after you move
into the palace. And I suggest you send one of the
boys after the truck. This damned stuff is heavy." She
turned on her heel and marched to the cockpit.

"You can't win with them anymore, amigo,"
McQuade confided. "I think they passed some new
law that lets them have things their way about ninety-
nine percent of the time."

"In America," Miguel amended.

"Yeah, well—" McQuade shrugged "—in that tape you said you were fighting for American-style democracy for De Colores. You're bound to end up with uppity women, just like that one."

Miguel shared a secret smile with McQuade as he watched Ronnie jerk the cockpit door open. "Your De Coloran woman is just as headstrong, my friend."

"What were the fireworks all about?"

"A government patrol trying to get a shot at you." He indicated McQuade's weapon with a jerk of his chin. "Would you care to shoot back?"

Miguel had no plans to send Ronnie back immediately. The plane had been fired upon this time. Seeing the troops take aim and knowing she was up there in that cockpit had filled him with rage. When the patrol had taken flight, his first instinct was to go after them. Instead, he had come to her.

Once they'd loaded up the assortment of automatic and semiautomatic weapons and the boxes of ammunition and explosives, Miguel fell in beside Ronnie and struggled once more with his instincts. He wouldn't allow himself any time alone with her. Not yet. Not until he was sure reason dominated his instincts once again. And he would have to plan for her departure, even if today was not practical.

Antonio was glad to see his truck. Chi Chi was glad to see McQuade again, and everyone was glad to see the new arsenal. Supper was served in front of the cantina, and even though rations were slim, there was a fiesta atmosphere. At the center of it all was the truckload of arms and ammunition, which was admired like a piece of metal artwork by everyone in turn. Families gathered with their children. Soldiers, some wearing parts of the uniform of the army they had deserted, clustered in small groups, discussing the merits of the new weapons and boasting of varying degrees of experience with them in the hope of attracting attention. Smokers shared cigarettes they'd guarded jealously. There was not enough of anything, but the *jefe* set an example of self-sacrifice that everyone was expected to follow. Observing it all, Ronnie shared an outdoor table with Miguel and McQuade, who were enjoying McQuade's cigarettes.

"*Bienvenida!* Welcome back, McQuade." Voluptuous Chi Chi with her bloodred hair sidled up to him from behind and draped an arm around McQuade's broad shoulders. "There must be some attraction for you here, since you keep coming back. What could that be, hmm?"

"Peace and quiet," he returned as he flashed Miguel a look of distress. "Nice place to get away from it all."

"Didn't you forget something the last time you left?" she asked sweetly.

He hadn't forgotten. He'd purposely left her standing on the dock while he and Elizabeth had made their getaway. "You don't want to go to Miami, Chi Chi." He gestured toward the yard full of men. "You've got everything you need right here."

"I bend over backward to help you and that skinny island *princesa*, and you repay me by leaving me behind." Her pout became a suggestive smile. "But now you're back, and you *are* the man of my dreams."

"Honey, you can dream all you want, but I've taken myself out of circulation. Permanently." He grinned up at her. "We're talking matrimony here."

"You *married* her?" Chi Chi pulled away in amazement. "That skinny—"

"Island princess. That's right. Didn't waste a minute after she said yes. Didn't want her to change her mind."

"*Que verguenza!* Such a shame, McQuade. I'm not interested in married men." She glanced at Ronnie as though sharing a bit of female wisdom. "They seem to lose their sense of humor when they get married."

McQuade chuckled as he watched Chi Chi join the crowd around Antonio's truck. "The truth is, they don't have to spend night after night pretending they're having a great time anymore," he muttered.

Miguel sent a stream of smoke into the evening air. "I have a plan that should put my forces on an equal footing with Guerrero's, and get you back to your wife within a couple of days."

"Oh, yeah? I have a feeling Guerrero's gonna be watching the skies for that plane now."

"Our next target is Guerrero's munitions dump. It looked like the only way to arm ourselves, and now, with the weapons you've brought us, we won't be committing suicide in the process. We'll take everything we can get our hands on and blow the rest up."

He removed his sunglasses, placing them carefully on the table, and looked at Ronnie. "Once we throw La Primavera into an uproar, you should be able to get away safely."

Ronnie nodded, hoping he wouldn't ask her for any promises. She saw too many needs here, and she couldn't promise to turn her back on them.

Miguel turned to McQuade. "I'll need your help, my friend. I know the layout, but I know very little about explosives."

The thought of sending Guerrero's toy closet up in smoke put a look of pure joy on McQuade's craggy face. "I'm your man."

Someone decided the weaponry windfall was truly cause for celebration, and celebration in De Colores meant music. Guitars, bongo drums, castanets and carved flutes began appearing in the grassy village square as a new white moon rose to brighten the starry sky. Antonio stirred up a rum punch, and soon people were singing and dancing to the island's traditional rumba rhythm. Watching them, Miguel let himself forget what had prompted the celebration and simply enjoy the cool night air, the scent of the sea and the sweet-tart flavor of the fruit drink. Soon he emptied his head of all but those sensations, noticing the way lilting strings and insistent drums combined to coax the hips to roll naturally, male courting female, female beckoning male.

Miguel looked at Veronica. She laid her cap on the table and ruffled her silky hair. The sleepy smile she returned assured him that her head was filled with all the same things.

"Let me teach you another dance," he said, and he reached for her hand.

The invitation came as no surprise to her this time, and she offered no premature apologies. The music felt like something elemental inside her, and it moved her toward Miguel. It moved her *with* Miguel. All others faded away. There was nothing but the night and the music and two who moved as one. Steady, rolling, undulating, the beat kept them moving, hip to hip, thigh to thigh, belly to belly. Approach, touch, slowly slide away, sway together again. The subtler the friction the more sultry the heat. His hips moved like lapping water, and her belly undulated easily in a feminine version of his fluidity. On and on and on rolled the pattering drum.

Dancing was so much like lovemaking that one gave way to the other with little more than a whisper. In a moment they were truly alone, hidden by the branches of a breadfruit tree. Under the onslaught of Miguel's kisses, Ronnie braced her back against the trunk of the tree and added inches to her height by standing on its roots. The undulating continued to the beat of the drum, thigh to thigh, belly to belly. He bent his head to kiss her breast through the ribbed cotton of her tank top, and when he sucked her nipple into a small, straining knot, she wasn't sure whether the groan it brought came from him or from her. She plunged her fingers into his hair and held his head fast, unwilling to let the pleasure his mouth brought her slip away. He lifted her top and suckled her other nipple until she gasped for her next breath.

Swiftly he unbuttoned her shorts, slipped the zipper down, and slid his warm hand over her belly. She whimpered, and he reversed their positions, supporting himself against the tree and cradling her against his shoulder while he kissed her face and sensitized her with his hand.

"Miguel . . ."

"This is for both of us," he whispered, his breath as hot against her ear as the place, that deep place his fingers sought and found.

"Oh, Miguel," she groaned, making an awkward attempt to unbuckle his belt. She was without dexterity. Her body was liquefying. In agonizing futility she rubbed her hand over the stiff denim and found him to be wonderfully hard.

"Shh, *querida*, shh. Let me take care of it for you. Yes, relax. Mmm, I want to feel you quiver in my hand."

"Miguel!"

"Ah, yes, *mi amante*, my lover. *Bueno*. It's good."

"Miguel." She sighed, and then they shared a long moment of quiet. She kept her eyes closed, certain that if she opened them she would feel foolish with what had just happened to her. "Don't you want me, Miguel?"

"Dios," he groaned. He took her hips in his hands and placed her firmly against him. "Feel how much I want you."

"What you did was beautiful, but...I would still..."

"*Querida*, don't. I cannot think with nothing but rum in my belly and my arms full of you."

"Why must you always think, always..."

"Because it's what I am good for." He combed her hair back with his fingers and kissed her forehead. "Tomorrow I will lead these young men on a raid, our first serious attempt at taking out an enemy advantage, and I don't know if I'm any good for that. If I'm not, I don't want to leave you..." She looked up at him, and he saw her fear. It reflected his own. "I don't want to leave you."

"Miguel..."

"You'll be here when I come back," he whispered fiercely. "This time. Just this one time. Then you'll go home to your little island and be safe."

"From you?"

"From all of this. When it's over...when this is over, Veronica..."

It seemed too risky to voice the promise, so he covered her mouth with his.

He took her to his room, gave her his cot and told her that he had to spend time with his men, especially the less experienced ones, to let them know that they could trust him to see them through the mission. Then he went out into the night, and in the privacy of a sheltered place near the lagoon, he gave himself relief.

*   *   *

The following day ticked by slowly. Miguel held strategy sessions with individual squads and with McQuade. Plans were mapped out in the dirt, and each squad leader was drilled on his assignment. Raphael was involved with much of the planning, and Paulo was an assault-squad leader. Everyone in the village had been assigned a job, and Miguel met with each group he'd organized, reminding them of their commitment, of the chain of command and of the contingency plan to take refuge in the mountains if the order should come. Ronnie had been assigned to the first-aid station, but Paulo came to her with news of another assignment.

"The *jefe* wants you to move your plane to a more sheltered place and camouflage it well." He touched the shoulder strap of his new M-16 automatic rifle and grinned. "I'm ready to escort you and show you the place he's chosen."

They walked to the airstrip, cutting across a sugar-cane field that had been devastated by the hurricane. "How dangerous is this mission, Paulo?" Ronnie asked as she adjusted the bill of her cap against the sun.

"The *jefe* has warned us that some of us may not come back. Everyone on the assault team volunteered for it."

"Why?"

The question surprised him. If she cared for the *jefe*, surely she knew why. "Because this will be the real beginning. Guerrero's only real advantage is that he is better supplied."

"That's a major advantage."

"Not *well* supplied," Paulo pointed out. "Just better supplied. Tonight we even the odds. Most of the men who have families chose to stay behind and defend our position. The rest of us—" He grinned with pride. "I was chosen because I've had training, and I know how to use this." He patted his weapon.

"And Raphael?"

"He will command the defense team."

Ronnie moved the plane as she was instructed, and she was satisfied that the new situation, away from the airstrip but with easy access to the cane field, was less visible. When she returned, she found Miguel in his room. A small arsenal was laid out on the cot, and he had dressed completely in black, right down to the combat boots.

"Come in, Veronica. I was beginning to think I would have to go looking for you. You've moved the plane?"

"Yes." Her voice sounded very small.

"Good." He took a pistol from a shelf above the bed and checked the clip as he spoke. "You'll leave with McQuade shortly after we've accomplished our mission. I don't want anything to happen to that plane."

When she said nothing, he turned to her and saw the reason. Her eyes were dry, but beneath the bill of that red baseball cap they were as wide as green saucers. At a distance she could be mistaken for a child, but there was no mistake when he took her in his arms and lifted the cap. This was his woman, whose version of his heightened sense of anticipation was pure anxiety. She would bear the burden of the wait.

He kissed her, and her throat burned with the sweetness of it. Then he took her face in his hands and searched her eyes for a message, something he could take with him that would supersede all words. "I want you safe, *querida*. I wish you could be home tonight having supper with Becky or maybe tinkering with your engine."

She managed a smile as she hooked her thumbs in the empty belt loops at the sides of his pants. "I wish *you* could stay and tinker with my engine."

"Be careful, *mi angel*. If that's an invitation, this is the only time I'll ever refuse it."

Her smile faded. "I want to go with you, Miguel."

"Don't talk like a child. You have a job to do here. Everyone has been..." He sighed and pulled her against his chest. "I couldn't do *my* job if you were there. As it is, I will worry about your safety until I see your face again."

"How long?"

"That depends on how they react. When you hear the explosions, you'll know it's half over." He drew away, touching her cheek with his forefinger. "Pray for us, Veronica. Your heart is as kind as your namesake's, and your prayers will be heard. Pray for a paintbox morning."

She watched him disappear into the trees in the waning evening light, and then she joined the others.

There was little talk. There was little to do now that everything was prepared. The night's silence became maddening. Then suddenly it was shattered by a series of deafening explosions.

Chapter 9

After the initial burst of explosions, it was hard to tell how much gunfire was exchanged. Staccato rounds were punctuated by more detonations. The people of El Gallo gathered in the square and encouraged one another, speculating about each ominous report. Government troops were on the run, they told one another. Ronnie nodded with the rest of them, but she knew that her smile was just as thin as theirs and her eyes just as bright with fear.

Raphael appeared suddenly, shouldering his rifle as he came to them from out of the darkness. "Get back to your posts!" he shouted. They stared at him as though they weren't sure who he was. "What are you waiting for? A direct hit in the center of town?"

Finding their wits, the crowd scattered. Before Ronnie could approach him with any questions, Raphael was gone. On her way back to the sandbagged root cellar that had been outfitted as an aid station, Ronnie chided herself for the foolish notion that Raphael would know anything more than she did. *When you hear the explosions, you'll know it's half over.* There was no turning back now. That was all anyone knew.

An hour passed. The explosions stopped, and sounds of gunfire became more erratic and were seldom close by. Three men were brought to the aid station, two with superficial wounds and one older man who was beyond help. Ronnie watched the light go out in the man's eyes and heard his wife's grief-stricken wail, and she felt numb. This was what the furious noise in the night was all about, she thought. This was what it brought. She left the aid station in a daze and headed for the cantina in search of more water.

"The first assault squad has returned!"

Ronnie turned toward the hand that had grabbed her shoulder and found it to be Raphael's. "Is Miguel with them?"

"No. They were sent back with a truckload of arms and ammunition. You should see—they got a bunch of stuff! They said everything went like clockwork, and the rest of our men should be on their way." Flushed with the excitement of his news, he flashed her a grin as he backpedaled away. "The fox got into Guerrero's henhouse, and the chickens ran for cover!"

Another hour passed, and two more vehicles returned with stolen supplies. Finally, all but eight of the men were accounted for. Miguel had sent his own squad back to the village in an effort to support the defense teams as quickly as possible, but it was becoming apparent that Paulo's squad had gotten into trouble. McQuade and Miguel were with them. The city's sirens could be heard, and an occasional gunshot, but the battle was over. Those who had returned were talking excitedly about victory, hedging only when the subject of the missing squad came up. For Raphael, who cocked his head at every sound coming from outside the perimeter of the village, the promise of victory had lost its sweetness.

Ronnie felt as if her nerve endings had all poked through the surface of her skin. Maybe they were pinned down somewhere. Maybe someone was badly hurt. Maybe some were trapped, and the others were maneuvering to free them. Maybe, maybe, maybe. Miguel was all right, she told herself. As the minutes ticked by, her prayers became more desperate. Bring them back. Bring them back. Her heart thudded with the words.

The small group straggled in just before daylight. Six shadows. Only six. Four young soldiers. McQuade. Miguel. Ronnie took several deep breaths and blinked back the burning tears before running to him.

She resisted the urge to make a fuss over his injuries, but as he dropped a weary arm around her shoulders, she took an instant inventory. None of the scratches looked serious. A blistering burn on his forearm would need attention, but the burden of his responsibilities obviously made him oblivious to his physical wounds. He pressed trembling lips against her forehead as she slid her arms behind his back. "How are things here?" he asked.

"One man died," she told him. "Carlos Denuedo. He had a chest wound, and there was nothing we could do for him." She tightened her grip. "Miguel, where's Paulo?"

Miguel's eyes met Raphael's as the young man approached. "McQuade," he said over his shoulder. "Find the other boy's family and tell them what's happened." He gave Ronnie's arm a gentle squeeze. "I must speak with Raphael."

Ronnie felt bereft when Miguel stepped away from her. The loss she had dreaded had not occurred, but she'd had only a moment to rejoice in that. Grief would descend with another loss, and she felt vaguely guilty about the relief she'd felt when she had identified Miguel in the group, as if no one else had mattered. Miguel spoke to Raphael privately, their faces only a few inches apart. He gripped the young man's shoulder, and Raphael nodded several times. Ronnie watched them walk away together.

Miguel found her waiting for him under the palm shelter near the Quonset supply building. She stood quickly as though her name had just been called for an appointment. He ducked under the fringe of dry palms and took her in his arms.

"Paulo's dead, isn't he?" she whispered.

"I don't know. He and another man spotted a rocket launcher and went back for it. They got caught. The last time they were seen, they were alive." He sat her down on an overturned crate and took a seat beside her. "I want to get you out of here just as soon as I can, Veronica, but I have to ask you to wait a little longer."

"That's no problem," she said as she took his hand and drew his arm closer. "You know I don't want to go, anyway."

"I need McQuade," he explained. In the dark she was trying to examine the burn on his arm, which he didn't remember getting. "If there's a way to get to them, McQuade will find it."

She looked up, her eyes glittering. "Just the two of you?"

"I can't stop Raphael from going with us. He needs to be in on it, for his own peace of mind."

"You don't sound hopeful."

"I think we'll find them." He sighed. "My greatest fear was that someone would be taken alive. I told all of them that."

She held his hand and let him sit quietly for a moment. She sensed his fatigue. "Let me take care of this for you," she whispered, touching his arm near the place where he'd been burned.

"When I come back," he said. "We need to leave now, before it gets light. Guerrero has more patrols out now. We didn't have much trouble getting in and taking what we wanted. It wasn't until McQuade started setting off charges that they really knew what hit them."

"Do you know where he might keep prisoners?"

"Prisoners." On the bitter sound of the word Miguel glanced away, and his voice grew raspy. "Paulo always tries to go one better. He's too impulsive." He shook his head. "I should have known better."

"He's been with you since the start, Miguel. You knew his capabilities. He told me that he had the necessary training and was familiar with the automatic rifle." She moved her hand to his shoulder. "He volunteered. He told me that, too—that you gave everyone a choice." She sensed that Miguel found no comfort in that fact. "At least you know they're both alive. When this is over, you'll liberate the prisoners. And then you can reprimand Paulo for his impulsiveness and send him off to school."

Her naïveté came as no surprise to him. She was an American, and in America even prisoners had rights. In De Colores, Guerrero had become the law, which was to say there was no law. There was only the ego of a madman. They heard the sound of footsteps in the grass, and they knew McQuade and Raphael had come for him.

He pulled her to her feet and gave her a quick, hard kiss. "We're going to move carefully," he promised. "Don't expect us back before midafternoon."

It was late morning when the three men finally reached the outskirts of La Primavera. It was as though an agreement had been reached to permit themselves a few more hours to believe in miracles. They had not been in any hurry to confirm what each, in his own mind, knew they would find.

The spectacle had been arranged at a gas station at the edge of the city. McQuade shoved his grief-stunned companions into the wreckage of a small hut in an overgrown, wind-battered orchard. He knew that Miguel would recover his senses in a moment, but the *jefe*'s heart ruled his first response. This was what they had expected—a scene, nevertheless, for which they could never have prepared themselves.

The bloodied bodies of the two boys were propped against the stucco wall of the gas station. Their hands were bound, and their heads lolled toward one another as though, even in death, they could somehow offer each other support. Their blood reddened the whitewashed wall. Two soldiers stood guard.

"I cannot leave them like this," Miguel said quietly. His voice was expressionless, his eyes hollow.

McQuade looked at Raphael, who simply stared. "This trap was set for you, Miguel. Take a good look." McQuade gave them a moment, but he knew both men saw only Paulo. "That's all we're supposed to see. Two bodies and two guards."

"Their bodies must not suffer further indignity, McQuade. We must spare them that."

"They're beyond suffering now," McQuade said gently. And then he cleared his throat and said matter-of-factly, "It'll be easy to take those two out. They're just kids. Sacrificial lambs. Guerrero can sure pick 'em."

Miguel nodded mechanically, still staring vacantly at the scene. "So can I."

McQuade's jaw tightened as he cursed himself for having taken the wrong tack. In about a minute he could see both of these guys throwing themselves on the pyre.

"I know that one." It was the first comment Raphael had made, and it came in a whisper. His voice grew stronger as he explained, "The small one. Ernesto Ramal. We called him Raton, the mouse. He always wanted to play center field, but the ball would fly right over his head." He gave a mirthless chuckle. "We made a good catcher out of him. Paulo was our best pitcher."

While they watched, a group of a dozen people came around the corner of a building about a block away. Men, women and children approached the macabre display reluctantly as though they had been shoved on stage. They huddled near the gas pumps and hung their heads. In the center of the group several people made quick, subtle signs of the cross, while those at the back cast furtive glances over their shoulders.

"The people are expected to desecrate the bodies somehow, but look—" Miguel touched Raphael's shoulder. "They refuse."

McQuade was interested in other aspects of the group's behavior. "That's where the big guns are," he whispered. "Behind that building." He surveyed surrounding roofs and saw no evidence of artillery. "Amateurs. I'd have put them up there."

After a moment, the people moved away. Another moment passed, and the man Raphael still thought of as Raton said something to his companion, who shifted his attention from the nearby trees to the quiet city street. While Miguel, Raphael and McQuade watched, the young man lifted the body of the friend with whom he had once exchanged pitching signals and laid him down carefully. Raphael stiffened when he saw the knife removed from the sheath on Raton's belt, but Miguel gripped his shoulder with a strong hand. They watched Raton cut the bonds from Paulo's wrists and carefully place his hands on his chest. With one hand he closed Paulo's eyes while he blessed himself with the other.

"That kid's no mouse," McQuade said softly.

Raphael's shoulder trembled beneath Miguel's hand as he dropped his chin to his chest. He gasped, strangling on his grief, struggling to stem the flow of his tears. Finally his shoulders sagged in defeat, and the drops fell on his thighs as he sobbed.

McQuade reached for the rifle lying forgotten near Raphael's knees. "Let's get out of here."

Ronnie made herself useful by helping to reorganize the first-aid station and fill more sandbags while she waited for Miguel's return. It was nearly nightfall when the three men appeared without the two they had hoped to rescue. No questions were asked. Miguel visited briefly with two more bereaved families, while McQuade sat under the thatched shelter with Ronnie and chose his words carefully as he recounted the events of the day.

"I haven't told Miguel this yet, but I've decided to hang around a while."

Ronnie stared at him. "What about Elizabeth?"

"When you go back, I want you to go see her. Tell her I'm okay and that things are looking good here. We have to move quickly now, before Guerrero can replace his losses."

"We need food and medical supplies."

"Hey, look, you're not part of that 'we.'" He caught the direction of her thoughts and grabbed her elbow, intending to nip her idea in the bud. "Miguel about had my head for letting you transport the guns. You're going home to stay, kiddo. For his sake."

The idea was well past the budding stage. "It isn't for you to decide what I need to do for his sake."

"I know how you feel about him." McQuade sighed. "Some guys love power, and they'll do anything they can to get it. If a few people get hurt, well, that's part of the game. Miguel's not like that. From the beginning he's been in this only because he thinks it's right."

"I know that."

"You've gotta understand, Ronnie. He just came back from seeing what was left of two kids Guerrero got his hands on. And Miguel was in command of the mission when they bought it. If anything like that happened to you . . ."

"I'm not a kid, McQuade. Neither was Paulo. He made a choice, and he was willing to die for it."

They saw Miguel, his face shrouded by twilight shadows, striding toward the shelter. "Tomorrow you'll do what you have to," McQuade said quietly. "Just don't add to his grief tonight."

Miguel ducked his head and stepped under the shelter. "They're serving supper in front of the cantina."

"Wonder what a shot of bourbon costs at La Gallina these days," McQuade said as he stepped over a crate.

"I think it's negotiable," Miguel replied. "Antonio likes to hear your stories."

"Antonio's one of my main men." McQuade gave Miguel's shoulder a parting squeeze. "Take it easy, amigo."

Miguel and Ronnie looked at one another as they listened to McQuade's retreating footsteps.

He looked tired, beaten.

"Have you had anything to eat?" she asked.

She was warm, vital, and he saw solace in her eyes.

"I ate something this morning," he said.

His heart was breaking. She felt it in her own chest.

"McQuade told me what happened."

Her heart was open to him. She offered sanctuary, but he felt completely undeserving.

"Both of them. They were so young." He lifted his hands slowly, palms up. They were empty, just as he was. "I failed them, Veronica. I should have been the one to—"

She stepped into his arms and held him. She would not deny his pain by refuting it, but she would not let him be alone with it.

"I should have been teaching them *about* wars—*past* wars, over and done—not asking them to join me in making this one." His chest sank away from her cheek as he snorted in disgust. "What do I know about making war? *Dios*, I'm a teacher. Just a teacher."

"You know about freedom," Ronnie whispered.

"Freedom? Yes, of course. Did I tell you about the villages we *liberated*? And now the liberated souls of young men who should never have been allowed to—"

"I love you, Miguel."

"What?" His voice was hoarse, and he looked down at her as though she had taken leave of her senses.

"I said I love you." He appeared not to understand, not to believe. "I can't give you back what you've lost. I can only tell you that you're a good man, maybe too good for the job you've assumed, because you care so much. And I love you."

In his despair, he could have turned it all back on her, refused to accept any of it, except the last. He saw himself as a presumptuous man who had already made too many promises, except to her. He'd promised her nothing, but she loved him anyway. He needed her beyond all reason.

"They've wounded you again," she said quietly.

His hands were in her hair, holding her head still while he searched her face for some reflection of his need. "You've mended me before."

"Let me try again."

His kiss was a plunging plea for deliverance from everything that ached inside him. He'd been afraid his lovemaking might hurt her, but she molded herself to him and welcomed him with an open kiss, telling him how much she wanted it. She would ease the ache. She would restore his health. She would take him, broken as he was, and make him whole again.

They went to his room. He closed the door, and there was almost no light. The louvered ventilators near the top and bottom of the outside walls permitted them to see the outline of one another. But Ronnie didn't need light. She knew this man. She knew the way his flesh quivered with pain or with desire even as his mind controlled his responses. She knew the sure, sensual way he moved his body when he danced, the way he led her, reassured her, accepted her responses and made her feel at long last comfortable with her femininity. She knew what to expect.

He peeled his T-shirt off and dropped it. When she moved to do the same, he stilled her hands and brought them around his back. "Allow me that pleasure," he said, and he slid his hands beneath her tank top, unloosed the back hook on her bra and ran his hands up and down her back, pressing her hips more firmly each time he reached them as he arched against her.

His skin felt warm, smooth and waxy from the heat. She kissed the curve of his pectoral muscle, and tasted the saltiness of him with the tip of her tongue. "Don't keep yourself from me this time," she whispered without lifting her head.

"I won't," he promised. He moved his hands slowly to bracket her breasts. "I can't." But he eased her away from him and swept his thumbs over her nipples while he kissed her as if her mouth could supplement the little food he'd permitted himself.

She groaned when his touch left her breasts straining almost painfully for him. "Raise your arms," he whispered into her hair. She complied, and he pushed both garments up her arms as though the act were part of a sultry dance. At the top of his journey he caught her hands and lowered them to his shoulders, letting the clothing fall. He pressed his lips against her temple, her neck, and then entered her hot, wet mouth with his tongue, holding her so that her nipples barely brushed against him. She felt spongy from the waist down, and she worried vaguely that her legs would not support her.

He held her under her arms as he lowered one knee toward the floor. "I'm hungry, Veronica," he whispered against her breast. "So hungry."

Literally, it was true. He took her nipple in his mouth and suckled, and she thought wildly of what satisfaction she would feel if she were able to give him real nourishment at her breast. She tunneled her fingers through his hair and only regretted the time he lost in moving his mouth from one breast to the other.

Then the waistband of her shorts went slack, and she felt his hard palms sliding over her hips, pushing the rest of her clothes out of his way. He knelt at her feet, freed her of shorts and shoes and then nibbled around her navel. He gripped one firm thigh in each hand to coax them apart. With his thumbs he teased her soft inner thighs, inching higher until she sucked her belly in with a quick breath.

Words of protest flitted through her mind like weightless moths chased by a steadily intensifying jet of need. He found the source of that need, and the jet shot to the place he touched with one deft thumb. And then he kissed her there.

He felt the bite of her nails in his shoulders, and he stroked her gently in return. He supported her inconsequential weight until he felt the fluttering within her that he promised himself he would prolong. Steadying her in one arm, he unzipped his pants and rose to his feet. He had a plan for putting her on the cot, but she caught him by surprise, caught his buttocks in her hands and pressed herself against him. Her mouth made a moist foray across his chest while she rolled her hips against him in a carnal rumba.

He followed her lead this time, their pulses providing the drumbeat. She slid her hands inside the back of his pants, maneuvering denim and elastic until he slipped his hand between them and freed himself. Her hand followed hard upon his, but when she found him, she hesitated. He guided her. "Don't shy away now, *mi amante*," he whispered into her hair.

But in a moment he knew he was nearing the limits of his endurance. He stalled her caresses with one hand and tossed his bedroll to the floor with the other. In another moment, all of his clothes lay in some unseen corner of the room, and he was cradling her, moving to cover her body with his. "I shouldn't do this," he whispered as the back of his fingers skimmed one breast, lingering lightly against the nipple he'd made round and hard, and then sliding over the tightly stretched satin of her belly. "*Muy hermosa.* So very beautiful. I shouldn't..."

She put her hand on his hip. "Don't shy away from me now, *mi amor.*"

He nudged her legs apart and moved between them, bracing himself over her and whispering of his needs in Spanish, the language spoken by his heart. Their bodies were slick with sweat. He whispered her name as he entered her, and she gasped. He thought he had hurt her and drew back, but she arched her back and held him inside her. He moved slowly, and she followed the lead he gave her. He groaned, wanting more, and she reached, offered, arched, gave. He moved faster, and she led the way this time as she left the weighty part of herself behind and soared on the declaration of her love. He cried out in pain and joy. She joined him in celebrating both.

And when he had spent himself inside her, he buried his face in the comfort of her shoulder and hoped she couldn't distinguish his sweat from his tears.

* * *

Ronnie found herself on the cot when she awoke.
She had no recollection of moving. She remembered
lying on the floor feeling pleasantly warm and sated
and safe, her arms and legs woven together with Miguel's, her mind drifting in sleepy satisfaction. In the
dark she listened for the sound of his breathing, but
the room was quiet. She slid down and felt her way
across the floor, but she found only a tennis shoe and
a blanket. In her groping she found her top but not her
shorts, so she dragged her bag out from under the cot
and dressed in the first thing that came into her
hand—her sea-foam dress.

She suspected the lagoon's tranquil water might
have drawn him to it the same way it lured her. The
night was warm and still, and the stars were dim-
ming. She stepped from prickly grass to soft sand. Her
heels scooped out footholds on her way down the
eroded bank. A cigarette glowed in the shelter of the
palms some yards away, and she padded across wet
sand in the direction of the small red beacon.

As Miguel watched her come to him he had a fleeting vision of her fanning the gossamer folds of her
skirt with outstretched arms and fluttering over his
head like a butterfly. He'd come to believe that she had
her own wings. He imagined her reaching down as she
passed, plucking him out of the trees and lifting him
high, carrying him away under the expanse of her
beautiful turquoise and jade wings. He shoved the
cigarette against his mouth and sucked the smoke deep

into his lungs. She was driving him crazy, filling his head with such wild . . .

"Is that you, Miguel?"

"Fortunately for you, *querida*, I'm not one of Guerrero's men."

She pushed past the fronds of waist-high vegetation and moved toward the shadowy form leaning against the trunk of a coconut palm. "If you're safe out here, then I must be, too," she said quietly.

"I'm not safe anywhere, but I did think to carry a pistol. Did you?"

"No." She stopped when another step would have taken her into his arms. "Why would I take a pistol along when I was looking for you?"

He turned his face from her and took a final drag on the cigarette. The smoke became part of the darkness. "Why, indeed?" he reflected as he dropped the butt and buried it in a hollow he'd scooped out of the sand with his bare foot.

"Have I done something wrong, Miguel?" She wanted to take that last step, but the distance between them suddenly struck her as a forbidding space. "When I woke up and found you gone I felt . . . I thought . . ."

He pushed away from the tree, took her slight shoulders in his hands and drew her against his chest. She sighed and slipped her arms around him inside his open shirt. His skin felt cool and damp. She found the pistol tucked into the back of his pants, and she flinched when she touched it. "Good grief, Miguel. If this thing went off, tending your injury would be a pretty indelicate proposition."

His chuckle came deep, rich and warm. "But I could trust you to work your delicate magic under the most indelicate circumstances." He kissed the top of her head. "No, Veronica, you did nothing wrong. In my heart everything we did felt perfectly right."

"And in your head?"

"My head," he reflected and made a clucking sound. "My head won't let me sleep. That's where my conscience seems to reside, and my conscience tells me that every moment I spend with you is a moment stolen out of your life."

"That's nonsense."

"Is it?" Even as he thought of putting her away from him, he crushed her closer. "Like Paulo, you risk too much, *querida*. Your life is too much. Do you think that being a woman or being an American or... or simply being too young to die makes any difference? Do you think you can't be touched?"

"I *have* been touched, Miguel." She tilted her head back and lifted her hand to his cheek. "I have nothing in my life that's more important to me than you are. You're worth whatever risk I may be taking."

"But I have—"

"I know." She touched his lips with her thumb and she smiled. "You do have something more important. I understand that."

"Veronica, it isn't—"

"Shh." She pushed her fingers into his hair and found that it was wet. "This is *my* time. Given or stolen, it's mine." She pulled his head down slowly and felt his body harden even as his resistance went soft. "Isn't it," she insisted.

"Yes." His mouth came down in a hard kiss that would deny her nothing. He caressed the soft skin bared by the deep vee in the back of her dress and speared her mouth with his questing tongue. He moved his hands over the frothy fabric, past her waist and over her bottom, and it excited him to feel the lack of anything but her beneath the dress. Sliding his kisses to her neck, he pressed her tight against him.

"I love this dress," he whispered as he slipped it off her shoulders. She freed her arms, and the bodice fell to her waist. As the night lifted toward day it pearlized her skin with a smooth, shining luster. Her breasts were like the mica-bright sand of his home. Their dusky peaks beaded under his scrutiny. He touched them, almost shyly. "When I first saw you holding this dress against yourself after you'd showered, I was torn between wanting to see you in the dress and longing for you to drop the towel."

She sucked in a breath at the thrill of his touch. "Ah, Miguel, what do you want now?"

"I want you again, querida. Here on the beach. I want to come into you just as morning breaks."

"That will be beautiful," she whispered as they sank together to their knees. He peeled off his shirt and put it aside with the pistol. She watched him slide his pants down his legs and saw only beauty in a body that was becoming too lean. He moved over her, and she touched first the bandage over the burn on his arm and then the puckered scar under his ribs. He gave tenderness for tenderness as he sought his place beneath her skirt. When he came into her, she turned her face to the bright red crack on the horizon and whispered, "Miguel."

He loved her well, with the coming of the light spurring him on. She rose to meet him, and the colors they mixed for one another brimmed, quivered at the moment of overfill, and then spilled over in psychedelic hues too intense to last. Replete, they lay in each others' arms and heard the sound of lapping waves, liquid color fading to warm pastels, soothing, soothing.

Miguel braced his elbow in the sand and admired her face while he spread her skirt to cover her thighs. She offered a languid smile. "Your hair is wet," she said as she touched it.

"I went for a swim."

Her hand trailed down his chest and rested at his flat belly. "You must eat more, Miguel. You make too many sacrifices."

He pulled the gathered fabric of her bodice to cover her breasts. "I was unable to make the one I intended where you were concerned. I need you more than food or sleep or... But I will not sacrifice your life, Veronica. I beg you to—"

She silenced him with a finger over his lips. The promise he wanted to extract from her would be impossible to keep. "Let's not miss the sunrise," she said.

He pulled his pants on, and she shrugged into the straps of her dress. The amethyst sky scattered gold dust and powdered rubies across the lagoon's winking ripples. For Ronnie it was an irresistible trove of treasures. They walked to the edge of the water together, but when he stopped, she kept walking.

The water buoyed the sea-foam dress in a circle around her hips and bathed her privately within that curtain. Miguel could hardly breathe as he watched her. The water loved her as he did. The sky laced her hair with glinting jewels and would lure her from him with the promise of more. Jealous, he waded in after her.

She met him in thigh-high deep water with her skirt clinging to her hips. Her face was filled with dawn light. "How's this for a paintbox morning?"

"You fill my heart with these colors, Veronica." He took her in his arms and lowered his head to her. "You fill me," he whispered against her lips. "You fill me."

At breakfast Miguel and Ronnie sat together with McQuade, Raphael, Antonio and others. Raphael ate quietly. McQuade offered his help in planning and executing the next raid, and Miguel refused it. Their discussion tied Ronnie's stomach in knots. McQuade insisted that they must press their advantage immediately, and that Miguel needed all the help he could get. Miguel wanted McQuade to return to his wife. Ronnie sympathized with that wish, but she wanted McQuade to stay. Miguel needed him. Yes, Elizabeth was her friend, but Miguel was fighting for the life of

his country. He had to let people take their own risks
if he were to stand a chance of winning.

She noted once again the scarcity of food. The hurricane had destroyed so much of the island's bounty,
and there was barely enough for two meals a day.
Beans, rice and fish, and none of it plentiful. They
talked of another raid, and she knew how depleted the
medical supplies were. She made her decision to leave
without telling Miguel. He would only try to make her
promise not to come back, and he would insist that
McQuade go along. It was a scene she wanted to avoid
because she had every intention of returning within a
day or two with desperately needed supplies. While the
men went round and round, Ronnie slipped away.

Miguel crossed the street on his way back to the
Quonset building. McQuade was right. His skills were
valuable, and put to proper use they could help bring
an end to the strife before the bellies of the children
became puffed with malnutrition. But he had to get
Veronica out safely. He would promise her the moon
and hope he lived to deliver it to her, but for now she
had to go.

She was not in his room. He reached for the dress
she'd hung on a hook earlier and let the soft, damp
cloth slide through his hand as he smiled, remembering. He was in for another argument, but his capitulation to McQuade was the only one he would make
today. And then he thought again how lovely she'd
looked standing there in the . . .

The explosion rocked him, and he was not aware that he filled his fist with fabric and ripped the dress off the hook.

Chapter 10

Miguel bolted for the door and scanned the tree line, his heart pounding in his throat. Black smoke rolled skyward from what he knew, with icy certainty, to be the cane field. He saw nothing along the periphery of his path as he ran. He heard nothing but the buzzing in his ears and, as he drew closer, the mighty whoosh of flames. He had a fleeting notion that someone else's legs must have been carrying him, since his were paralyzed with fear. When he saw the wing tip, the tail and the ball of fire, a terrible, anguished sound ripped his throat.

Flames licked furiously at the Cessna's metal body. The cockpit had become an incinerator. McQuade shouldered his rifle and tore across the field. Miguel was running blind, a senseless moth headed for the flames, shouting, "Veronica!" McQuade managed to tackle him, bringing them both to their knees in the stubbled field. Heat rolled across the ground in waves.

"They've killed her!" Miguel clawed at the earth as he struggled to free himself. "My God, they've killed her, they've killed her, they've killed her..."

"Take it easy," McQuade pleaded as he hooked an arm over Miguel's shoulder and dug his heels into the ground. "Take it easy, amigo. How do you know? Maybe she wasn't in there."

"I was looking for her," Miguel panted. "I couldn't find her. She was gone. She was..."

McQuade felt the man's chest sag beneath his arm. He loosened his hold and squinted up at the raging fire. "You can't see a damn thing in there. There's no reason to assume... We've gotta back off now, before she blows again. C'mon!"

McQuade half dragged, half carried Miguel to a safe distance. As if on cue the auxiliary fuel tank exploded. The plane was blown apart, and pieces of metal scattered in all directions. The two men watched, helplessly mesmerized.

By twos and threes the villagers ventured forth. They knew their job. The defense measures that had been planned were put into action as the fire-fighting teams organized their efforts to keep the flames from spreading. Miguel stood silently and watched while his heart shriveled and burned before his eyes. The people lowered their heads in respect for his grief as they moved past him.

"We'll search for her, Miguel."

McQuade's voice seemed to come to him through a long tunnel. Miguel nodded dumbly.

"By the looks of it, I'd say they either tossed a grenade into the cockpit, or—" He sighed. He hated the second possibility. "They could have wired the ignition with a detonator."

"In which case, someone turned on the ignition and set off the charge." Miguel's voice was hollow, and his eyes were glassy.

"Yeah." McQuade squeezed Miguel's shoulder. "I'll...probably be able to figure out what happened when the wreckage cools off."

"I'm interested in only one piece of information." He turned to McQuade in dark anguish. "If she'd been anywhere in the area, she would have come running when she heard the explosion."

"We'll look for her."

Miguel knew the search was hopeless. He also knew that Ronnie would never have regarded it that way, so he searched, praying all the while for some sign of her and some piece of her optimism. He found neither. He had no tears. Tears were triggered by the heart, and he had watched his heart die in those flames. Those who loved him tried to console him, but he saw little and heard nothing. His mind spun like a child's top, and his chest was a cold, empty cavity. Finally there was only McQuade to keep the vigil with him in the waning hours of afternoon under the rustling palms of the shelter.

"You know we're going to have to hit our next target tonight," McQuade said. He picked up a stick and drew a line in the dirt at their feet. "We decided on the control tower at La Primavera airport. We should be able to get the job done, like you said, without civilian casualties. While they clean that mess up, we go for the harbor patrol headquarters, take out a few patrol boats." Miguel stared at him, and McQuade wondered whether he'd been heard. "Hell, I know it sounds callous, Miguel, but either you strike now or you lose your advantage. There'll be time to mourn them all properly when this thing is over."

"I want Guerrero," Miguel said in a flat, even tone.

"We'll get Guerrero," McQuade promised. "We go about this right, we'll have him inside a week, guaranteed. Nobody's backing him. Every day a few more of his regulars come crawling out of the woodwork and ask to join us."

"I want him dead, McQuade. I want to put his corpse on display the way he did Paulo."

Miguel's threat was so quiet, so deadly that it nearly masked his grief. "You'll get your chance," McQuade promised. "You'll have his head on a platter. And then it'll be up to you to dispose of it—" he waved his hand at the range of possibilities "—any way you want."

Miguel's face became murderous. "You think I won't do it?"

The anger was good, McQuade thought. It was better than the catatonic state the man had fallen into earlier. McQuade studied his friend's face. "I think you won't do it. I think you're not like Guerrero."

Miguel pointed to the ground. "If I had him groveling at my feet, defenseless and begging for mercy, I would cut his heart out."

"That's fair," McQuade said quietly. "That's what he's done to you."

Miguel's shoulders sagged, and he gripped his knees. It all seemed like such a nightmare, an absolute absurdity. Everything around him looked just as it had yesterday, but nothing could ever be the same again. He'd loved her and lost her within a matter of hours.

"I loved her, McQuade. She gave, and I took, but I loved her." Miguel turned his head slowly, and the pain McQuade saw written on that lean, dark face made him shudder. "What kind of a man lets his woman die without telling her he loves her?" Miguel asked.

"A man just like the rest of us, amigo." McQuade laid a brotherly hand on Miguel's back. "She knew."

"I wish—" His voice went hoarse, and he had to start again. "I wish I had told her."

The airport control tower went up in flames along with two cargo planes. Within hours, the harbor patrol headquarters was a pile of rubble. Miguel's men cleared people out of the target area while McQuade set the charges. During the next two days Miguel's men kept government troops on the defensive. Small bands of Miguel's guerrillas hampered every retaliatory effort by the city-based government troops, and the villagers protected their own. Striking repeatedly without allowing Guerrero time to regroup was paying off. And it was the single objective of Miguel's every waking hour. The prospect of defeating Guerrero kept him sane.

McQuade watched Miguel toy with a shot of the bourbon that Antonio protected like a hoard of Liberty dimes. It wasn't just the one glass of bourbon Miguel was considering. McQuade knew the look of a man who was mulling over the prospect of getting drunk. Miguel certainly had the look, and no one deserved a few hours of oblivion more than he did. They had run out of cigarettes, and there was little else for consolation. In Miguel's condition—tired, hungry, emotionally twisted at the center of his gut—a couple of shots would be all it would take. But McQuade knew Miguel wouldn't do it. In a moment, he would push the glass aside and talk about tomorrow's raid.

At the sound of the back door creaking open McQuade dropped his hand on the M-16 that lay on the bar.

"It's Antonio," Miguel said confidently.

McQuade was ready to shoot if it wasn't. Antonio saw McQuade's reaction as he entered the cantina from his apartment in back, and his eyes were momentarily a bit rounder than usual. They looked at one another, and then everyone relaxed. Doubt was a sign of the times.

It was a gray, rainy afternoon. Antonio reached for a towel to dry his head. "I have news," he announced as he rubbed the back of his neck dry. He turned up the flame on the kerosene lamp so that the two men might appreciate every nuance of his tale. "Chi Chi's friend Juanita, who lives in the city now since the storm ruined her house— You remember her, Mc-Quade. She did some errands for you."

"Yeah, I remember Juanita."

"Well, she was in touch with Dorothy Bartholomew at the Red Cross office in La Primavera, and she relayed a message to you—through me, of course." Antonio's eyes shone with his pride in being recognized as McQuade's contact.

"Dorothy's still around?" McQuade scowled. "Damn. I'd hoped she was safe and sound in the States by now."

"What's the message?" Miguel asked impatiently.

Antonio preened with the distinction of carrying a secret for important men. "It comes from Mikal Romanov. He says Freedom International is working for you. They have put together a report on Guerrero's activities, and the State Department is listening. He also says that Guerrero is getting nowhere with any government in his requests for military assistance."

A smile spread over McQuade's face. He looked at Miguel and saw nothing but cold satisfaction.

"It's good news, isn't it?" Antonio asked.

McQuade slapped Antonio on the back. "It's good news, my man. It means Guerrero is no more flush with ammunition than we are."

"It means we pick our targets carefully and end this nightmare as quickly as we can," Miguel added.

The front door opened, and Raphael stepped inside, also dripping wet. He, too, had news. His eyes were bright with it, but there was neither joy nor sadness in his expression—only excitement. He pulled a brown envelope from under his shirt and held it up. "A package from Guerrero. It's for you, *jefe*."

Miguel reached for the package, but McQuade got to it first. "Just let me check this baby out first," he muttered as he tested the envelope with uniquely perceptive fingers.

"Guerrero doesn't have the finesse for such delicate plotting, McQuade." Miguel sipped his bourbon and watched McQuade treat the envelope with studied care. He was almost amused. "I suspect he dreams of pulling the trigger on me in person next time."

"Ain't gonna be no next time, amigo." McQuade slipped the envelope's flap off the clasp and peered inside. His face dropped, and then his features froze.

"What is it?"

McQuade looked up and passed the envelope to Miguel as though it were, indeed, something that might blow the roof off the cantina. He bit his lower lip as he watched Miguel take a look, then reach inside.

With an unsteady hand he drew out the envelope's precious contents. A red baseball cap sporting the Boston Red Sox logo in a size that would accommodate a wealth of silken hair and a small, delicate head. The envelope fell to the floor.

"Who delivered it?" McQuade asked as he bent to retrieve it. "What did they say?"

"The man knows nothing, *señor*. He's just some terrorized merchant who is doing what he was told to do. He's supposed to return with a reply."

"Guerrero's probably holding the man's wife until he gets back." McQuade found a note at the bottom of the envelope. Without further comment he handed it to Miguel.

The words blurred on the paper when Miguel first held it up. Still clutching the cap, he laid the note next to the kerosene lamp on the bar, smoothed it out and willed his eyes to focus.

"It says they have her." The words danced mischievously in front of his eyes, and he wondered if they teased him deliberately. "It says...it says she's alive."

"What does he want?" McQuade asked.

"How do we know he's telling the truth?" Raphael put in.

"It could be any cap," Antonio added.

Miguel turned, his eyes alight for the first time in days. "It isn't *any* cap. It's *her* cap."

"That doesn't mean she's alive," Raphael said bitterly.

"It doesn't mean she's not," McQuade returned. "It just means they blew up a plane and got a baseball cap out of the deal. Maybe more." He turned to Miguel and asked gently, "Does he say what he wants?"

"He wants to talk. He says that I am to meet him at the gas station—the one where they had Paulo—at a time of my choosing. He will bring Veronica."

"Alone?" Antonio asked.

"I am to be alone."

"He won't be," McQuade said.

"*Jefe*, it's a trap." Raphael stepped closer. "Just like it was before." The *jefe* didn't seem to hear him, so he took another step. "You might find the same thing you found before. It's no good to see that, *jefe*. You'll hate yourself if you walk away, and if you don't . . ."

"I'm going to find out whether she's alive."

"How do you propose to do that?" McQuade demanded.

"We're going to take the palace, McQuade. We're going to end this thing."

"If they've got her, they'll kill her for sure if we try anything."

"I'm going inside." A thin, humorless smile reflected Miguel's mood. "In my mind I've gone over a plan for taking the palace a hundred times. Every detail. We do it by getting a team inside first. Only now there is an added detail. That team must get Veronica out."

"If she's there," Antonio insisted.

McQuade exchanged a hopeful look with Miguel. "We'll know soon."

"I need paper," Miguel said quietly. "Our merchant must be returned to his wife. Guerrero can plan on a meeting tomorrow. We will plan our strike for tonight."

He penned the message in a bold, even hand. Let Guerrero believe he would walk into this willingly, anxiously. The belief would be short-lived. He handed the note to Raphael. "Send an escort with this man, and tell them he is not to reach the city before nightfall. Antonio, I want you to bring me all our squad leaders."

As the two men headed out into the rain, McQuade took note of the distant look in Miguel's eyes. The *jefe* needed some privacy. "I wanna check supplies," McQuade said. "I'll be back for the meeting." He laid a hand on Miguel's shoulder and offered his customary, "Take it easy, amigo. I've got a strong hunch she's okay."

"I like your hunches, McQuade."

When the door was closed and the cantina was quiet, Miguel allowed himself another look at the red baseball cap. Hard-boiled as he was, McQuade was blessed with a touch of that American optimism, Miguel told himself. Not as generously endowed with it as Veronica was, but it showed through at times like this. It was almost tangible. Miguel liked the airy feel of it. Optimism. *Dios*, he could fortify himself with the taste of it and get through the next twelve hours on nothing but that, but the specter of Paulo's battered body would not leave him alone. He pressed the bill of the cap over his eyes and silently begged the awful image to go away.

The litany of her name became a hoarse chant as he rubbed the well-worn cap over his face and savored the scent, the feel, the slim but precious chance.

* * *

Miguel's plan depended on stealth, timing and teamwork. He knew the palace well. During the time he'd been there, he had taken an interest in its structure and its history. It had been built in the seventeenth century to house the Spanish viceroys. Remodeled many times over the years, it featured a whole system of hidden rooms and passages once used to conceal valuables and to protect inhabitants from any number of threats—storms, pirates, even rebellious De Colorans. This time the tables were turned. The palace's chief occupant had no interest in its history or its secret passages. The island's chief rebel did.

Miguel assigned Raphael and six small squads to the assault on the palace. Each had a primary and secondary target. The squads would converge once inside the walls. After disabling two sentries, Miguel led a seventh hand-picked squad over the garden wall. Now each man had his job to do. Two of the men who had once been palace staff would hit the armory while two others took out the two machine guns that were mounted on the roof. McQuade followed Miguel as he picked his way through the neglected tropical foliage that had once been a carefully tended garden. Their objective was underground.

Miguel paused between two palmetto palms, still dripping from the rain that had ended earlier, and looked around to assure himself of his bearings. The big cedar had fallen against the wall, but this was the spot he sought. The palmettos and the mango trees sheltered them from being viewed from the palace.

Miguel began ripping the new growth of creeping vines away from the clay tile. He uncovered a handle and pulled open a wooden hatchway, which was tiled to match the rest of the terrace. Miguel followed the barrel of his rifle down the stone steps. When he reached the bottom, he flicked his flashlight on. McQuade joined him, closing the door behind them.

The passageway was cool and damp and smelled like fertile humus. An array of creatures, most of them heard but not seen, scurried for cover as the two men worked their way along the route that Miguel hoped only he and these creatures had recently explored. They came to a fork in the passage. Miguel pointed to the left. They passed a room, and Miguel flashed his light on a cache of kegs and bottles, hoarded by some Spanish connoisseur who had long since stopped aging. There were other rooms along the passage, but Miguel showed no interest in them. His sights were set on another set of stone steps and another trapdoor that led to an obscure storage room in the east wing. If Guerrero were holding a prisoner whose stay would be short, Miguel suspected that she would be kept in that wing, perhaps even in his old office.

Miguel pointed his flashlight at the steps and ran the beam up to the underside of the trapdoor. McQuade nodded, and they retreated along the passageway to the fork.

"This tunnel adjoins the sewer system." Miguel's hushed voice echoed softly. "The grate is directly under the front gate. I'll try to get her back to the tunnel before the charge goes off."

"If she's here," McQuade reminded him.

"Yes. If she's here."

McQuade gave a thumbs-up sign and headed down the dark passage. Miguel adjusted his rifle strap on his shoulder and hurried back to the stairs. The hallway was dark, but one light shone, and one sentry was posted near the door to the office suite Miguel had occupied in what seemed another lifetime. The sentry had to be guarding someone, and Miguel prayed that it was Veronica. If Guerrero was behind that door, he was a dead man.

The sentry turned his ear toward the door. "You need what?" he said. "I'm sorry, but I can't—" The young man gave a disgusted sigh and took a ring of keys from his pocket. Miguel pulled his pistol and moved closer. The soldier pushed the door open and stuck his head into the room. "What? No, no, I've made them as loose as I dare. The general assured you that this situation would only be tempor—"

Miguel struck the man over the back of the head, then stepped over the fallen body and into the room, his finger on the trigger of his weapon. In the next second he nearly dropped it.

"Miguel! My God, how did you—"

"Shh." He touched a finger to his lips and fought back blurring tears. She was tied to a chair, but she was alive. His angel was alive! He dragged the soldier over the threshold and closed the door. He dealt first with the bonds on her wrists. Her arms were stretched diagonally across the back of the wooden chair, with each wrist tied near the seat. He cut the ropes, but she couldn't make her arms move right away. Her bare feet were tied to the front chair legs. As the ropes fell away he tried not to think about the rope burns on her ankles that matched the ones on her wrists. He couldn't coddle her now.

"My arms," she whispered.

He looked up quickly and immediately wished he hadn't. A red welt underscored her right eye, and she grimaced as she tried to rotate her shoulders. "How bad?" he asked.

"I don't know. I've been sitting like this for so long."

"Do you think anything is broken?"

She shook her head quickly, but she really didn't know. Her arms protested her every movement with bone-splitting pain. He put his hands on her shoulders and massaged gently, and she groaned. "Try to get the circulation going, *querida*. We must move quickly."

He gathered the rope and moved to the unconscious sentry. "Did this one hurt you?" Ronnie shook her head. Setting his pistol within easy reach, Miguel quickly bound and gagged the man and dragged him into a closet, muttering, "You'll sit this one out."

Ronnie stood up slowly and flexed her ankles and her knees. "Come on, blood," she ordered, trying to ignore the rush of dizziness she was feeling. "Get pumping."

Miguel laid his hand on her shoulder. "We must move quickly and quietly. Are you able to manage?"

"Yes." She had to be.

"Can you use this?" He offered his pistol.

Sort of, she thought. I can't hit anything with it, but . . . "I know how to fire it."

"Good. Stay close."

He led her through quiet halls to the storage room. He removed the false floor covering and opened the trapdoor. "This is one avenue of escape," he whispered in the dark. "It leads to the garden, which will probably become a dangerous place in a few moments. You should be safe in the tunnel, but not in the garden. Not unless I come for you."

"What's going on, Miguel?"

"We're about to topple Guerrero's house of cards. McQuade is setting a charge under the gate. When that goes off, the attack begins."

He guided her away from the secret door and took a position facing the door to the hallway. He wanted to hold her, but he had to keep his priorities straight. His rifle was aimed at the door. The things he wanted to say to her would have to wait. If he started on them now, the rifle would soon be forgotten.

"Did you think I was in the plane when it blew up?" she asked in a voice that was barely audible.

"Yes," he answered tightly.

"I almost was. Then somebody decided I might be useful."

"Does Guerrero know . . . what is between us?"

She swallowed hard. "I don't think so. He just knows I brought you the guns."

"Did he . . ." This was not the time to ask, but he couldn't stop the question. "Did he hurt you, *querida*?"

"No, not . . . not really. He hit me and threw me around a little. I don't know what he thought I knew. How did you know I was here?"

Miguel's hands tightened around the grips of the automatic rifle. "He sent a messenger. He wanted me to meet him."

"He would have killed you."

"He would have killed both of us."

The explosion rent the night, and Miguel smiled to himself in the dark. It had begun. One blast followed another—on the roof, in the courtyard, in the west wing. He could identify them all by direction. The sound of footfalls on the stone steps made Ronnie stiffen. Miguel turned the rifle toward the trapdoor. "McQuade?"

"I think I really made a mess of your gate, *jefe*," was the answer from below. "Did you find her?"

"She's right here."

"She okay?" McQuade stepped out of the hole, clicking off his flashlight.

"I'm fine."

"Hiya, kiddo."

"Hiya, McQuade."

"So let's not let Raphael's boys have all the fun," McQuade quipped. "Let's see if we can find the snake's head and chop it off."

Miguel took hold of Ronnie's arm. "You are to wait at the foot of these steps. Anyone who comes for you will identify himself when he opens the door. If he does not, be prepared to shoot him."

"I'd rather go with you, Miguel."

"You were not in on the planning, Veronica." He pressed his flashlight into her hand. "Please do as I say this time."

"I will," she whispered. "I promise."

In total darkness he found her lips instinctively and gave one brief, hard, desperate kiss. Then he pushed her toward the secret door. "Don't use the light unless you have to. I'll come back for you myself if I can."

Ronnie found her way to the bottom of the steps and stood there for a moment, blindly trying to make sense of where she was. She didn't like it. It smelled like wet clay, and the air felt clammy. She ached all over anyway, and now the dampness crept into her bare feet. Above her she could hear gunfire, and she shivered. Dying, darkness, death. Was this the way it felt to be inside a tomb? Something ran over her foot, and she decided she wanted to be buried with her shoes on. She didn't want to be buried at all—what was she thinking? This was awful. Musty, dusty, surrounded by earth. She was a sky person! When she died, she was definitely going *up*.

She couldn't stand the suspense any longer. She flicked the switch and shined the flashlight beyond the steps. A tunnel, a scurrying squad of mice and a hole in the wall. She clicked the light off. This was hardly the Hilton. Maybe they could call it Catacombs Inn. Air-conditioned niches for a never-ending night's rest.

Oh, God, people were actually shooting at people up there. Miguel was up there. Guerrero was up there.

Guerrero. That bastard. His best feature was the big red scar next to his left eye. The rest of his face was ugly and devoid of any spark of human emotion. Except when he was inflicting pain, she amended, and then his eyes were anything but human. She had tried to hit him back, but he had found her efforts amusing. She had seen people strike others before, and their eyes were always full of some combination of anger and fear. Behind Guerrero's fist Ronnie had seen black eyes gleaming with demonic pleasure. During her encounters with him, Guerrero had made it clear to Ronnie that the man he wanted most was Miguel Hidalgo.

Ronnie's whole body stiffened as her mind formed pictures of destruction for each explosion she heard. At her back, the earthen well shuddered with the rumble of man-made thunder, while behind her eyes bricks and mortar crumbled, and human bodies became part of the debris.

After what seemed an interminable time, the trapdoor was thrown open. Ronnie stuck the flashlight in her pocket and stepped back, holding the pistol in both of her trembling hands.

"Veronica, come quickly!"

She lowered the gun, took out the flashlight and mounted the steps. "You're supposed to identify yourself."

He laughed. "It's Miguel."

"Miguel, Miguel, Miguel," she chanted as she raced toward heaven. Her flashlight illuminated the hand he extended to her. "Miguel who?" she squealed as she grabbed his hand and sprang from the bowels of the earth into his waiting arms.

"Miguel Hidalgo, leader of the De Colores Freedom Fighters and rescuer of—" They shared a kiss in celebration, and he ended it with another joyous burst of laughter. "Beautiful, beautiful women," he finished.

"Is it over?"

"The fighting? Yes. We're searching the palace room by room, but Guerrero's troops have surrendered. We haven't accounted for him yet, but there are bodies yet to be—" He smiled when he realized that she was trying to check him over while he talked. He knew he must look like the devil.

"You're okay?" she asked.

He leaned down until his lips were close to her ear. "I can't be certain until my angel of mercy gives me a thorough examination. But that will have to come later."

"You're bleeding here," she said, touching his chin. "And here."

He closed his hand around hers and kissed her fingertips. "In turn, I intend to examine you. Are you all right?" She nodded, and he touched the bruise under her eye. "The thought of this makes me crazy," he said quietly, taking the flashlight from her hand. "I have a safer place for you now. We've secured the central offices."

They moved into the hallway. Dark and quiet, it seemed to be in a separate world from the distant shouting and the occasional gunshot that could be heard outside the building. Miguel doused the light and took the lead. When he rounded the corner at the end of the hallway an attacker charged out of the darkness, and Miguel's rifle discharged as it clattered to the floor. Ronnie stumbled backward, and something brushed her foot as it sailed past. The attacker and Miguel became entangled in one grunting, pounding, thrashing ball of fury. Ronnie had the pistol, but all she could see were dark shapes. It was like watching two men struggle inside a huge sack.

The flashlight! She had felt the flashlight hit her foot. She groped along the floor, cringing at the sound of bone-breaking combat. She knew well the sound of Miguel's voice, but she heard nothing that resembled its rich, smooth tone. The two men snarled like wild beasts. Their furious, incoherent shouts seemed to lend power to the body blows. Finally Ronnie's hand struck metal. She pivoted on one knee and edged closer. One hulk rose above the other, arm upraised.

"Miguel?"

"Get back, Ver—" The arm came down with a thud.

Ronnie flashed the light in the face of the towering figure.

His eyes were glowing coals, fires undaunted by a mere flashlight beam. In that split second he seemed to enjoy her challenge, although he could not see her face. The red scar mocked her. He knew she had a weapon pointed at him but that she dared not fire it. The man she loved was too close. With nostrils flaring, he savored the smell of her fear, and delighted in her dilemma. He knew she was afraid she'd miss. He knew she was equally afraid of hitting a human target.

Then his eyes popped with shock. He peered into the light in disbelief. His thin lips parted, but no words would come.

"Diablo," Miguel hissed as he came up from his knees. He got a better grip on the knife he'd pushed into Guerrero's gut, and jerked it upward. The fiery eyes went wild. Guerrero gasped, and finally the devil's fire was extinguished.

Ronnie brought the light closer. Standing inches from Miguel's back, she could feel the trembling aftershock that racked his body. He drew several deep breaths, each one more controlled than the last, and then he took the flashlight and knelt beside the man he'd killed. The pistol dangled in Ronnie's hand. The hilt of the knife and the spreading red pool looked surrealistic at the edge of the circle of light. Ronnie thought she might have been watching a movie, except that she could smell the warm blood.

Footsteps echoed in the hallway. Ronnie touched the pistol to Miguel's shoulder as another flashlight beam rounded the corner.

"Jefe!"

Miguel dropped the lifeless wrist. "It's all over, Raphael. We've severed the snake's head."

* * *

The following day announcements were made. Rodolfo Guerrero was dead. The news was greeted with apprehensive silence. Miguel Hidalgo had once been dead, too, many of the people grumbled among themselves. Who could be trusted in times like these? The people were tired and hungry and past caring who lived in the palace as long as it was someone who would let them clean up the rubble and reopen their shops, get their boats back into the water and replant their small fields.

The villagers knew Miguel Hidalgo better than the city people did, and they helped spread the word that the reign of terror was over. Restoring order occupied Miguel's time and energy immediately. Guerrero's top aides were held in custody, and the island people breathed a tentative sigh of relief as they turned their efforts to rebuilding. Miguel sought emergency food and medical supplies, and relief agencies responded quickly. The constitution would come, the elections would come, but first he would staunch the flow of blood and feed his people.

The first shipment of supplies arrived from the United States within hours of the call, and Ronnie and McQuade were on hand to help Dorothy Bartholomew of the Red Cross set up aid stations and arrange for the distribution of food. The two were assigned the happy task of making the first delivery to El Gallo. They stood aside while Antonio and Chi Chi supervised the unloading of crates of powdered milk and eggs, farinha and Florida oranges.

"Breakfast is served," McQuade observed with a satisfied smile.

"Orange juice." Eyeing the Florida-stamped crates, Ronnie could almost taste her favorite drink. "Did you get hold of Elizabeth?"

The sound of the name made his eyes light up, and he nodded. "She'd already heard the news, and she and Tomas are on their way. She wants to help." He shrugged. "I guess it'll be sorta like doing a little stint in the Peace Corps. Hell of a honeymoon, huh?"

"Are you complaining?"

McQuade's grin completely erased his hard-boiled image. "If that woman wanted to honeymoon in Antarctica, I'd be shopping for snowshoes. How about you? Did you get through to your family?"

Ronnie nodded. "My dad was quick to point out that the insurance on the plane won't cover an act of war. Looks like I'll be working for someone else for a while."

"You going back?"

She nodded again.

"What about Miguel?"

"What *about* Miguel?"

"Nothing. Just that the man's crazy about you."

She looked down at the toes of her gym shoes. "Miguel has a lot on his mind now. When the new government gets organized, he'll be president. That sort of puts a different color on things, doesn't it?"

"What color is that?" McQuade asked.

She lifted her chin and gave him an incredulous look. "*President* of a country, McQuade. Presidents don't get crazy over charter pilots who wear high-topped sneakers and baseball caps.''

"So change your shoes.'' The stars in his eyes told her that nothing could have been more obvious to a gumshoe who'd just married an island princess. "Listen, you see that little hut over there?'' Ronnie turned her attention to the house he pointed out. "That's Tia Teresa's place. She's pretty antisocial, and she probably won't get in line for any of this stuff, so I'm gonna take the mountain to Mohammed. She helped Elizabeth, and I owe her more than a few oranges. So that's where I'll be when you're ready to head back.'' He smiled and gave Ronnie's shoulder a friendly tap with his fist. "Don't change a thing, kiddo. Get yourself a new baseball cap. Miguel loves it.''

Ronnie pushed her fingers through her hair as she watched McQuade walk away. She would, she decided. She would get another baseball cap, but not because of Miguel. She needed it to keep the sun out of her eyes and her hair off her neck. It was practical. She was practical. And it was time, for once in her life, to be realistic, too. No president was likely to choose her to be his lady.

Miguel found her walking barefoot in the lagoon's white sand. Tan shorts, a salmon-colored tank top, and strawberry blond hair unfurled by the breeze were framed by rippling water glistening in the afternoon sun. The urge to put life's less pleasant demands aside and simply become one with Veronica was almost overwhelming. He had believed that she was lost to him, and he had never known such a feeling of emptiness. He started down the sandy bank and realized how uncomfortable his shoes were, so he pulled them off and left them lying in the sand beside his socks. With a sense of weightlessness he picked up his pace.

"I believe you dropped this, *señorita*."

Ronnie turned on the axis of her heart and found the promise of her own brand of heaven beaming at her through brown eyes. "Miguel!" She curbed her impulse to throw her arms around him and managed a little laugh. "You're forever popping in on me out of nowhere. I didn't even hear you walk up." She glanced down at the hand he held out to her. "Oh. My baseball cap." She reached for it as though she doubted its authenticity. "Where did you find this?"

"A man brought it to me thinking I might know its owner."

"Thank you." She studied the red cap, fingering its brim. "Funny, isn't it? The things we get attached to. My dad took me to Boston once. He asked me what I wanted to see most, and we looked in the paper. I picked a baseball game. He loves baseball." She looked up. "What do you think he'd have done if I had told him I'd always wanted to see a ballet?"

"I can only tell you what I would have done."

"You would have taken me." She smiled. "Always the gentleman."

"I would have taken you because you wanted to go. Had I asked you what you wanted to see most, you would have told me honestly." She glanced away, and he touched her arm. "Whether it was a baseball game or a ballet, you would have told me, wouldn't you?"

"Yes."

"Why?"

"Because... because you're too much of a gentleman to laugh at me either way."

He took her shoulders in his hands and made her look at him. "Because your happiness is important to me, *querida*. Your safety, your happiness...and your honesty. Why are you leaving me?"

She looked up at him in surprise. "Leaving you?"

"I came looking for you, and all I found was McQuade. He told me."

"Oh, well...in a few days, a week, whenever things settle down a little. I know there's a lot to do around here, but, of course, sooner or later I'll have to figure out what I'm going to do about—"

"I asked you why you're leaving *me*."

A hundred questions went unanswered in the looks they exchanged. Ronnie smiled bravely. "Maybe because you're too much of a gentleman to lay the cards on the table yourself."

"I'm not a cardplayer, Veronica. I'm a teacher. I prefer discussion."

Still clutching her cap, she laid her hands against his chest and spoke to him as softly as the quiet water splashing against their bare feet. "You are an important man with a very important job to do. You haven't had a moment for yourself since...since we—"

"Forgive me," he said just as softly. "I thought you understood. I should have—"

"No, I *do* understand, Miguel. What we had here in this quiet spot was very special to me, and I don't ever want you to apologize for it."

His brow beetled as he stared down at her. "You told me you loved me."

Her throat went dry, and her reply was barely audible. "I do. But you don't have to worry—"

"Worry? I never know what you're going to do, *querida*. I can't help but worry. You fly through enemy fire with a planeload of guns and explosives. You sneak away while I'm not looking, your plane goes up in a pillar of flame, and I die inside while I watch. When they brought me that cap and the hope that you were alive, I thought I might live again, too." He touched the fading bruise beneath her bright, teary turquoise eye. "I nearly went mad knowing what he was capable of doing, knowing he had you. I'm sorry for all you've suffered on my account."

"It wasn't your fault," she whispered as a tear slipped to her cheek.

"It wasn't my intention. It wasn't what I wanted to give you. I didn't say the words because I was walking around with a huge target pinned to my back, and I had no right to love you. But I did. I do." He pulled her into his arms, and her tears were warm against his neck. "I love you, Veronica, and if you leave me, you will take the color from my life."

She hugged him with all her strength because her throat was full of tears and her heart was bursting. How else could she answer?

"I'll run for office, and I'll serve if it be the will of the people, but don't ask me to do it alone, *querida*. Don't ask me to do it without my angel. Before I met you, my mornings were gray."

"I don't believe that," she managed, half laughing, half crying.

"It's true," he insisted, leaning back while she lifted her face. "I was a stodgy old professor—bookish and totally unaware of the beauty, the many beauties... You're so beautiful. Tell me, Veronica. Say the words to me."

She smiled through her tears as she put her baseball cap on his bookish head. "What words?"

"The words that sound like gold and vermilion and every shade of blue in the Caribbean." He brushed his lips against her forehead and whispered, "Let me hear you say them, Veronica."

"I love you, Miguel."

Epilogue

Mikal Romanov followed his son, David, down the steps from the airplane. Mikal's wife, Morgan, was in the lead. This trip to De Colores was the family Christmas present, and Morgan had promised herself that *this* time she would actually get to enjoy the white sand and blue-green sea. The last time Morgan had visited the island, she'd had serious business to accomplish with the three men who'd been holding Mikal and her father hostage, but this time she was there for pleasure. They had left North Dakota's two feet of snow behind them for ten days, and Morgan was anxious to break out the suntan lotion. Mikal smiled to himself at the prospect of slathering it all over her. He had pleasure in mind, too.

"So what's the big grin for? You think we'll see any action down here this trip?"

"Action?" Mikal laid a hand on David's shoulder as they walked across the runway. David had a new look. Huge black-rimmed shades and long hair. Mikal loved it. It reminded him of the sixties. But he was afraid to ask what a fourteen-year-old boy's idea of action was these days.

"Sure. This place is like one headline after another. Maybe we'll get attacked by a gang of crazed Ninja dwarfs or something."

"Or maybe we'll attend a fairy-tale wedding and everyone will live happily ever after and absolutely nobody will drag your father into a crisis for the next ten days." Morgan Romanov slipped her arm into the crook of her husband's elbow. "You didn't leave any phone numbers, did you?"

"I told Uncle Yuri—"

"Oh, no."

"—that we were going to Tahiti."

"He'll almost believe that," David put in sarcastically.

"Mr. and Mrs. Romanov?" A young man stepped forward and offered a gracious smile. "I am Raphael Esperanza. President Hidalgo asked me to meet you. He said to tell you that your old room at the palace is waiting for you and that your son will have special accommodations."

The look Mikal gave Morgan made her blush.

* * *

McQuade lay stretched across the bed, his head propped up on a cocked arm, as he watched Elizabeth arrange her satiny black hair. His wife was the fairest in the land. The mirror in front of her could not lie. She was dressed in the same pale-pink dress she'd worn for their own wedding, and he felt just as awed by her now as he had the day she had exchanged vows with him. He still couldn't quite believe she was his.

"I'm glad you were able to get Tia Teresa to help with Tomas," Elizabeth said. "There will be so much to celebrate at the fiesta tonight, and I haven't danced in years."

"You mean I'm supposed to be able to dance?"

She turned, hands on hips, and gave a coy smile. "You did check dancing on the application, Mr. McQuade."

"You mean the application for the marriage license? I was so nervous, I checked everything."

"I certainly hope you didn't falsify any qualifications, *Mr.* McQuade." She sat beside him on the bed. "It would be such a disappointment to discover that I didn't get what I bargained for."

He laughed and reached for her as he rolled onto his back. "I'll dance your shoes off, lady. Then I'll toss you over my shoulder and haul you back up here so I can get what I bargained for."

"Boorish American." With a contented smile, she plucked at his T-shirt. "You'd better get dressed. We have a wedding to attend in less than half an hour."

He grinned. "How about another advance?"

Elizabeth McQuade lowered her head and happily allowed her husband to kiss her lipstick away.

Ronnie wished she could call the whole thing off. Miguel had told her she could have any kind of wedding she wanted, and she wished now that she had suggested a small ceremony in the palace chapel. Instead, she had planned a big public occasion, and now she had to face the music. The garden had been refurbished and was now in full bloom. The flames of a thousand candles were mirrored in the reflecting pool, and the guests were waiting to witness a wedding.

There was a knock at the door. "Are you ready, Veronica?"

"Al-almost." She took another hard look in the mirror. She'd probably overdone the blush. Yes, she definitely had. She looked like a clown. She snatched the last tissue from the box on the vanity. The rest formed a heap between the array of makeup and the brush and comb.

"May I come in, *querida*?"

"No!" She didn't want him to see her. "Yes." He was the only person in the world she wanted to see.

He opened the door and stuck his head into the bedroom they would share that night. It was not his room, but one he'd designated the honeymoon suite because it was on the third floor and would give them privacy. He'd furnished one of the alcoves as a dressing area for her, and he could hear her movements but he couldn't see her. "You're not going to leave me standing at the altar, are you?"

She stepped into the room and took his breath away. Her dress poured the colors of the Caribbean over her body in a soft, feminine style that reminded him of a vintage forties film. She'd told him she'd decided against white in favor of a more flattering color, and she had chosen his favorite. Her hair was full and soft, and her lips were pink, glossy and ready to be kissed by her adoring groom.

He closed the door behind him, and she wondered if anyone so handsome could possibly be real. His black hair and dark tan were startlingly beautiful with the ivory tuxedo. His brown eyes glistened, and it occurred to her that she might be the cause.

They drank each other in.

"You look beautiful," they said in unison, and then each gave a nervous laugh. They stood several feet apart, uncertain about the next move.

"I'm scared," she said.

"So am I."

"They're all waiting, aren't they?" He nodded. "I should have let Barnaby give me away."

"You wanted to come to me on your own," he reminded her. "The way you always have."

She nodded, remembering how she'd planned it before she knew how scary it was going to be. "Becky fixed my hair," she said. "How does it look?"

He swallowed. *"Bello,"* he whispered, and then found a bigger voice. "Beautiful."

"Miguel, let's get the priest to come up here and just . . . marry us right here."

"That would be fine with me, but the priest might take exception." He smiled. "It was your idea to share our celebration. The next time I kiss you the fireworks will be real, not just in my head." He reached out for her hand, and she smiled as she laid it in his. "The idea is a good one," he assured her. "The people need a celebration. I just need you. You and your wonderful paintbox."

Hours passed before Miguel had *just* Veronica. After they had made promises, he had kissed her before all the world, a kiss that triggered a burst of fireworks and cheers throughout the city. They accepted all the good wishes and feasted and danced until the merriment was well underway. And then they slipped away.

They whispered more promises while they made love, and when they were too contented to do anything but lie in each other's arms, they pondered the night's wonders. The doors stood open on the balcony, and the fireworks display continued for their entertainment. Bursts of gold glitter and showers of pink stars adorned the canvas of night sky. The drums and guitars played dance after dance, and the air was filled with the voices of people enjoying life.

"Four years," Miguel said quietly. "Maybe eight, but I hope someone can be found to replace me after one term. Then I can be myself again. Professor Miguel Hidalgo. I want to build a small college here on the island."

"And we can go on that research expedition."

"By that time, we'll have to take the children."

"Mmm." She turned her head to plant a soft, wet kiss on his chest. "I don't know how I'll be with this first lady business, but I'll make a terrific mother."

"Making you a mother is my job." She nibbled at him, and he groaned. "And you have slipped into the role of first lady quite satisfactorily. Ah, look at the sky, *querida*!"

She turned in time to see the crackling splashes of blue, green, silver and gold. "That's how it feels when you make love to me," she said. "Those are the colors you make inside me."

"I promise to color our nights if you'll paint the mornings."

"It's a deal," she said, moving over him. "Get out your paintbox, *mi amor*."

* * * * *

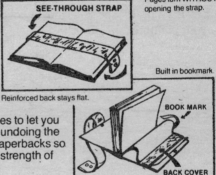

1989
IS THE YEAR
OF THE MAN!

What makes a romance? A special man, of course, and Silhouette Desire celebrates that fact with *twelve* of them! From Mr. January to Mr. December, every month has a tribute to the Silhouette Desire hero—our **MAN OF THE MONTH!**

Sexy, macho, charming, irritating . . . irresistible! Nothing can stop these men from sweeping you away. Created by some of your favorite authors, each man is custom-made for pleasure—*reading* pleasure—so don't miss a single one.

Mr. January is Blake Donavan in RELUCTANT FATHER by Diana Palmer
Mr. February is Hank Branson in THE GENTLEMAN INSISTS by Joan Hohl
Mr. March is Carson Tanner in NIGHT OF THE HUNTER by Jennifer Greene
Mr. April is Slater McCall in A DANGEROUS KIND OF MAN by Naomi Horton
Mr. May is Luke Harmon in VENGEANCE IS MINE by Lucy Gordon
Mr. June is Quinn McNamara in IRRESISTIBLE by Annette Broadrick

And that's only the half of it—
so get out there and find your man!

Silhouette Desire's

MAN OF THE MONTH . . .